Call Me Sweetheart

Call Me Sweetheart

Sean Houston

Sean Houston

Call Me Sweetheart

© 2020, Sean Houston

Self-published

ISBN 978-1-7356297-0-4

Preface

"Man cannot remake himself without suffering, for he is both the marble and the sculptor." It was always the latter part of this Alexis Carrel quote, somehow in my consciousness, that I had known. I had adopted it as the mantra for my bodybuilding journey. It was many years later that I discovered the first half of the quote, and that someone had already put my feelings into words. I started thinking more about this idea of suffering, and change. When I set out to write my novel, I knew where I was going, and I always knew where it was going to end. I never wanted to write a novel where the story arc follows a protagonist having missteps, but then figuring things out entirely and coming out on top. Instead, I wanted to write about all of the struggle and suffering—doubling down on bad decisions with more bad decisions—and I wanted it to be as real and raw and honest as possible. I chose to write in a very sexual, and unforgiving light, and wrote about a time I had reeked of desperation in this life so intensely that you could smell it on me. One simply cannot wash off such desperation; its lingering effects are much like handling freshly-cut onions barehanded. When one finds themself in such a desperate state, failure and deleterious decision after deleterious decision can be the norm. I found my decisions left me completely lost in an ocean of carnal pleasures. And I almost drowned, for I thought I had grabbed hold of a life vest in these casual encounters, when I had actually grabbed an anchor.

Beneath the surface of sex, there is a far darker subject. Throughout this novel, there is an undercurrent of depression and suicide. I had always viewed suicide as this inevitable thing. I don't mean in a romantic way, but as this terrifying vague feeling that was never too far away from me. The best way I can describe depression is that it's a room without any light. Not just darkness of night, but a place where light doesn't exist—a place where nothing should be able to survive. It is a place where heaven doesn't seem possible, because hell is all you know. Every once and a while in my life, however, there would be faint glimpses of hope in the form of possibility— someone new to give affection to. But how do you connect with a person? I had always been able to make friends easily, but when it came to that next step of a meaningful relationship, it always felt out of reach. When I would try opening up to people in the past on a deeper level—whether it be family, women, or even friends, it was difficult, and I found myself more often than not feeling rejected. Even in the company of others, I felt profoundly alone. For a long time, I thought there was something wrong with me. I became completely dejected about it. I craved love so deeply growing up, and I was working hard to make my mom and stepdad proud, but that acceptance was never there in the way I needed. They resented me a lot of the time it seemed. Even with this resentment, I still craved their affection. I wanted to be accepted by them. It just didn't play out that way, and I was kicked out. Despite that stressful beginning, things started looking up for me. I found myself liking the responsibility of living alone, and the newfound freedoms and time to myself. But in my isolation, that vague feeling grew in intensity.

And so, I ended up moving into a house with a friend, and everything seemed to be lining up in my life. I didn't have a girlfriend like I had wanted, but I felt a certain sense of peace. This was short lived. The time I wanted to meditate and work on creative things and to improve my life, slowly became invaded upon by my roommate— who gradually turned into a raging alcoholic. I didn't know how to leave, or how to help him, he didn't want to change, and I never considered saving myself. He was dangerous, and I didn't want him to know me—the real me. This didn't feel like unfamiliar territory at first, and so I stayed there longer than I should have. As a result, this was a slow, soul-eroding time, but I felt as if I was out of options. I had been treading water for a while, and I was so damn exhausted that I felt like I couldn't do it anymore. Every nerve and instinct I had told me to run away, but instead, I went on a trip to Georgia, where I was born. I wanted to visit my father to try and sort things out in my life. He must have felt that vague sense of impending doom as well in his life, as he made his share of mistakes. By the time I had tried to reconnect with him, he was in jail for a non-violent crime. I was able to talk with him on the phone and spend time with his family, but I didn't get the catharsis I had hoped for. I managed to keep things together on this trip, and part of me wishes I had stayed there, or at least not driven back to the black hole I found myself in. I was at the peak of my depression. It felt like my whole life was a problem without an answer. I remember getting into my car one night and accepting that I was going to end my life. I had no purpose, no place to put all my love, and no home. I had a place to sleep, but nowhere that I felt welcome or felt that I could be myself. I drove around to places I grew up, to places I spent time with friends, past the houses of girls I loved. Finally, I came to my parents' house. I wanted to go inside and hug my mom, and tell her that I wanted to know her, but on the condition of being accepted for who I was. I wanted us to have the relationship we had both always needed. Instead, I drove past and drove miles away. I had no particular destination in mind, but I knew what was coming. On the way back to the roommate's house in Steelton, going sixty miles per hour on the highway, I crept up to seventy, then eighty, then ninety. This is it. This is the end. And I let go of the steering wheel.

Something happened. By some kind of divine intervention, the instinct to survive took over. I was meant for something more. The next week I walked into my doctor's office, tears streaming down my face, and said that I needed help. The anxiety and depression were too much. I was prescribed Wellbutrin, and I started taking the medication. I began to feel better about my life. I was spending my nights jogging down the streets of Steelton, and lifting weights at home, and soon I moved out on my own again. I still wanted to connect with someone so badly, as a way of distancing myself from that vague feeling—even though things were improving, that feeling still lingered. I felt the best way to achieve this connection would be to lose a lot of weight, to make myself more desirable to women, and to openly pursue them sexually in the hopes that I could eventually give them love, and maybe have that love returned. I knew women were physically attracted to me, but I had so many more daydreams of the idea of having women to love and love me, that I never thought about sex as a means of getting that love. The cliché is that men lure women in with promises of love, only to have an ulterior motive of a one-night stand. My sinister plan was the opposite. I had an overflowing river of affection that I withheld under the guise of a hookup. I became very good at giving pleasure—so good that I thought this was my purpose in life. I thought at some point that if I could please them enough, then surely they would return the emotional affection I desired. In my darkness of depression, I pushed myself to the limit with pursuits of the flesh in trying to find a place for this love. I woke up one morning remembering a fact buried in my mind—that the stomach of a carrion bird has such strong stomach acids that it instinctively seeks out and is able to digest even the harshest and most rancid sustenance to survive. I found myself existing in life in a similar way, subsisting on the most basic crumbs of love I could gather. I realized I had to do more with my life, and that I had to make good on the debt of being saved—this is when I started writing.

So then why did I write a novel at all, and why write it so vulgar, and why so dark? Perhaps there isn't a place for writing such a novel, but my vision was always to say something honest no matter how ugly or pathetic. I wanted to say something beautiful out of the ugliest things. I believe art is a form of truth, and the greatest thing an artist can and should do, is to be truthful. It is also possibly the single most important quality and capability a person can have—to speak their being, their essence, in an honest way. To be able to speak what's in your heart is a part of being free. This is what really happened with me, and I own it. As I began to write my story, I thought more about the idea of re-making oneself, and the necessity of suffering. All that pain I experienced—that agony of a tortured and lonely existence—it was always leading me to work on myself, even if I didn't know this at the time. When I began working on myself, I found the courage to go to my parents, and to forgive them. As it turns out, they worked on themselves too. As I kept working on myself, I found I had so much untapped strength. And as I've grown strong enough to take care of myself, I now have the strength to help others, too. There are other people struggling, also in dark places. And maybe all it will take is the courage of one person to be vulnerable enough to lead the way out of darkness. It doesn't have to be this extreme of an example of suicide, and perhaps it won't ever manifest in a way in which you can articulate your type of despair. It may be hard now, but take it from me—there is no darkness too great to come out of. Even the most irredeemable of us not only deserve a shot at redemption, but we can achieve it if we work towards it.

When it comes to mistakes, missteps, and difficult times in life, it can be hard to see a future. It can be daunting to think of the possibility of trying to improve your life, and the idea of failing can seem so gargantuan that it seems monolithic. That's why it's important to start small. The sculpture starts as a whole block of marble, and takes a long time of slowly chipping away to reveal itself. Self-improvement takes just as much time and effort, if not longer. But you are worth the effort. It can be a challenge some days, but remember as you work on yourself that there are good things in life. There is light at the end of the tunnel, and things do get better. There is something beautiful out there for you, over the rainbow there are blue skies, beyond where you might be able to see today. You will have many weak moments before you're able to be strong, and you may need a lot of help along the way, and that's okay. You are strong if you are here today, and you'll only grow stronger as time passes. You can outlast the pain. If I can connect with and reach even one person with this message—be it through this introduction, or my novel—and save a life, it will be worth every ramification that can come with writing such a novel. It may seem at times as if there are no answers to your challenges in life. But I believe that you too, are meant for something in life. My purpose brought me in life to write these words. Herein lies the secret to life— we all have a purpose. This isn't to say that everything happens for a reason, or other such vague platitudes. But we all have a purpose. In my search for meaning in life, I found a number. Science tells us that each person has a 1 in $10^{2,640,000}$ (that's 2,640,000 zeros) chance of being born exactly who they are, and that the probability of a life-sustaining planet is somehow smaller. Science gives evidence of the impossible reality that we are all miracles. These kinds of odds don't exist on accident, and neither do people. You defy probability, you are wonderful evidence of purpose. I cannot tell you what your purpose is in life, only that you have one. It is out there, waiting for you to find it. It's important to know you matter in this life, and it is your life to live. So live your life, live your life, live your life.

Darkness

"Mmmmm, you can do that as much as you like," Savannah whispers in a soft moan, "we should do this all the time."

"I want it all the time, like right now" I start to lick and suck on her clit again. She already came softly, not as much wetness as I like, but she still tastes perfectly semi sweet—and I can see her hands reaching down to spread her pussy, egging me on to suck on her clit, and I oblige. In between her moans I find myself having to taste inside her, and I lap up inside her pussy, but I'm getting frustrated as she keeps resisting as I lift her legs to lick her ass too. I feel her convulsing, close to orgasm yet again, and I start sucking even harder on her clit, moving my head from side to side. Getting animalistic, my tooth brushes up against it accidentally—as her pussy juice is spreading all over my face as she cums again. I move up to her lips, wanting her to taste herself on me, and I start kissing her. She's giving me mixed tongue kisses, wanting them but thinking that it's too intimate. At first, she's resisting my finger slipping inside her, not necessarily because of her tightness, but because she thinks what she wants is sensuality. Our lips continue touching—in soft lingering pecks, and although she's closing her legs slightly on my fingers, she's relaxing more as I start fingering her G-spot. It's just one finger at first, but I quickly segue into two. Like most girls, the closer I get her to a G-spot orgasm, the more resistance she gives, as it's new territory for her. I can't blame her though—most girls don't even know what it is, and some are embarrassed by the mess they make. But I crave it all—their lack of control, the mess, the dizzying lust afterwards that slips in to falling in love for a brief moment.

"Don't just leave the kiss right away." She says, even though I'm kissing her in this tender, lingering way.

"I'm sorry." I say, unsure of what to say—

2

what she wants me to say.

"Well just relax. This feels... forced..." she says. We're cuddling now, which is nice, because I'm exhausted.

"You're right, I'm sorry. I just have a hard time relaxing when I have coffee, I probably shouldn't have had that cup of coffee earlier." She's saying goodnight, and that she had a great time, and that we'll set up a second date, and that she'll text me. There's an insatiable urge to love a woman inside me, to listen to the sound of their voice, to feel their breath on my neck, to know what's on their mind, to have their intoxicating perfumes and pheromones fill my nostrils, to explore their bodies and witness the trembling and convulsions of orgasms that show all at once who they are as a person in a beautiful moment... I'm texting her the next day and I never hear back from her.

Nights With Strangers

"Yeah keep looking over here, nigger. That's right, look away, fuck you." This black woman is shooting daggers at me as I pretend to not notice that she's calling me a nigger just slightly above her breath. I'm standing inside the Capitol Diner waiting to pay. "That's a capitol idea," I would always say, whenever it would be suggested for a late night snack.

Walking out with a friend, I say softly "man that table was fucking unreal," and we both chuckle, which is a relief from the tense half-hour of the loud drunk hollering we endured across from them. After walking over to his car and saying goodbye, I make my way back to my car and notice the same woman from earlier standing by her SUV, which happens to be parked next to my car.

"Are you mad honey?" She says, with drunken sadness spilling over from inside her being.

"What? Oh, no... I'm just really tired."

"Cause you know how it goes when you're drunk, and out with friends, you can get a little loud and crazy."

I don't know, but I agree anyway "Yeah, yeah I understan-"

"I noticed your body in there." She cuts me off mid-sentence, blurting out this confession as if I were a school crush.

"Well come right over here and feel this bicep," I say as I make a muscle, which makes her wince with shock as she feels it. "I work very hard on my body." I look right in her eyes as I'm saying this, making her tremble with the eye contact.

"I can tell... ooh and your chest is nice too." She's massaging my chest muscles without asking. This is almost too easy, but when she gets a call on her phone I start my car, too bloated from diner food to even consider spreading her legs at her place. "You sure you aren't mad baby?"

5

"No trust me, you're fine, really." I drive away, regretting not staying with her longer, winding up at her place, being a hazy memory in a hangover. My hand starts thumbing my cell phone in my pocket, I'm removing it and turning it on to see if I have any text messages. When an ocean of sadness washes over me at having none, I choose to ride the wave and go driving through the areas I grew up. I'm driving down roads that lead to ex-girlfriends, to feel them again if only through the presence of the sacred ground that they were on. My heart starts sinking, and feelings of intense loneliness that I don't want to feel rise to the surface, so I take my Wellbutrin, unsure if I've already taken one today. And I begin prowling Craigslist again, at 2 A.M.

"Hey guys I'm here in Harrisburg looking for a gentleman to get a room with me for the night." I respond to the ad with my usual nude picture (slyly covering up my cock, my body better in it then than it is now) and a "Hey there ;)". I don't

6

want to be thinking or feeling, and I don't want to be with someone that is either. I just want a random hookup to replace these emotions... Maybe I can fuck the pain away, fuck the pain away...

"Do u have a pic of ur face. R u a giving gentalmen?" She writes back after a few minutes of me refreshing my email.

"Sure, here you go, and I'm very, very giving :p" I check my wallet, and am thankful that I have three hundred dollars there.

She writes back, "U a cop? U have to tell me if u are. Im lookin 4 200 gifts." My hard-on, which was throbbing, now starts to fade away, but I still try to salvage it.

"No, I'm not a cop. I am, however, a security guard on the weekends. Just so you know for future reference, that is a myth by the way. Cops aren't obligated to tell you they're cops. And yeah, $200 sounds reasonable."

"Wate, now i dnt trust u. ur actin suspisious. I didnt say ne thing about money" I'm almost completely soft at this point, and I don't know what's worse: the fact that I realize at this point there's no way she's even remotely attractive, or her horrendous spelling.

Completely frustrated, I type back, thinking on my toes, "Okay... fine, I will have 200... roses. ;)"

"Roses? Yea i like that"

"Okay, well so where are you then? I'm feeling very giving, and I kind of really want to give you a massage, and well, you know :p" She gives me the address, a Days Inn on Eisenhower Boulevard, which I quickly make my way to. "I'm here then, where are you?" I write her.

"In my room. . ill come out." I casually walk around the lobby, and I'm somehow sobering up from my horniness. My mind tries to tell me, naggingly, "Hey, this could be a sting operation you

8

know," but my cock still aches, and I turn off my mind again. I'm leaving the Day's Inn not having gone through with it, disappointed by how she looks, and I make better use of my free time on dating sites. I have a familiar face to a lot of the girls on there—of a father who didn't give them enough love, or an old boyfriend who abused them, someone they want to earn redemption or love from. I'm driving down the highway, narrowly missing other drivers, sending out semi-generic messages with a handful of questions about their profile peppered in to show I read through it. I message on average fifty girls a day, easily, sometimes even a hundred, every day. When I run out of "matches" I just expand the search area, sometimes up to 200 miles. "Eh, yeah I would drive that far for a blowjob." It's easier to just take a Gatling gun approach, spray and pray, than to deliberately court one person and be let down if it doesn't work out.

I have another message from a girl who is

available today, without any requests to break in the relationship. She has a certain look that says she has potential to be a great girlfriend, but that she's also very kinky. She stated on her profile that she was going to another country to be a missionary, and that was all I needed to know. I'm laying with her in my bed, kissing her. "I don't normally kiss guys." She chuckles and goes on to say, "Sort of one of those rules. The last date I went on, the guy tied me up and threw me in his trunk and left me there for hours. I was so turned on the entire time. I begged him another time to tie me up naked to the front of his car. He did, and it was the fucking best." I keep trying to kiss her, to feel that spark, but her lips are like a deep well— whatever humanity and soul in her is just so deep down, that it's only a soft echo of a sound. "We can't have sex because I'm on my period, unless you wanted to go down on me? I know some guys are a little weird about it." I wrinkle my nose for a second, thinking about it.

10

"Well how would that even work?"

"You know, you just have like a glass of water there to spit it out of your mouth if you don't like it."

"Hmm, why don't we just do things on our next date!" I say with a jubilant smile, so naïve to not realize this is it. This is always it. As she looks around the room, she's deciding in her mind that she's somehow ashamed she was ever here, that somehow I'm beneath a faux abductor. She's starting to talk about her upcoming trip to Haiti, where she'll be working as a missionary. That she needs to fight her urges, and that the trip should help.

"I'll text you." She smiles, as she forgets how my door opens up, looks around nervously, and leaves. I'm texting her later and I don't hear back from her. It's over, and the search for a replacement of a replacement continues.

Cat

Now I'm talking with Cat, and everything about her says "doormat". She looks desperate in the football jersey in her profile picture, screaming "see how much we have in common?" to most men. Our first "date" is at the guard shack where I do security at. "Oooh, are you going to have to restrain me? ;)" the girls would always say, as if they actually thought they were cleverly the first to say it. I like the honesty they show in such playful banter, and I like that like myself they're barely containing their slutty nature. She comes to me, with a little too much makeup on, and she really wants me to want her. "What do you think of my makeup?" She asks, with her neck cocked ever so slightly to appear more feminine.

"I love the way your eye liner looks."

"I was hoping you would notice that, I remember you saying how important that is to you." Her tongue is in my mouth, and mine is softly caressing hers. My hands are down her leggings, and I'm grabbing her thick ass, looking at it naked as I pull back her leggings. I can actually feel the change in humidity from her wetness. "That's as far as we're going tonight. I like you, and I want it to work out."

"Okay, I think I like that."

She's at my place for our second date, and asks to use the bathroom after we make out a little bit. I can see her giving herself a pep talk in her head: "No, nothing's going to happen tonight." But we both know she's already powerless. We sit on the couch in the living room, and I'm telling her to straddle me, which she does. She's removing her bra as I'm squeezing her ass, and out comes these wonderfully pink, perfect 19-year-old nipples. I start sucking on them, and she's moaning loudly as she starts to grind into me. Something's not working right on me though, I'm not getting hard at all. The only thing I can think of is the Wellbutrin— I took an extra pill today that gave me a severe headache. A memory came floating back, of my grandmother laying in bed, looking so frail and weak at the end of her life... saying that it was okay, that she was ready to die, and how it crippled me. Soften it up... take another one, it'll all balance out I told myself. Anything to put that memory away again.

My headache is subsiding, and I'm taken over again with a carnal desire to make this young girl cum in a way she didn't think was even possible. I throw her on to the couch, man handling her. I peel her panties down, she hasn't shaved in a few days—her legs, or her pussy. It's a light, lumen-like, blonde angel hair. I know it's because she wanted another barrier, to stop anything from happening. I hear her say softly "Sorry I didn't shave."

"Shh," I say, reassuring her. I start licking inside her pussy, I can taste the traces of urine from when she went to the bathroom earlier. I can feel that she's self-conscious, so I put her at ease

14

and start tonguing her clit, and I'm fingering her pussy at the same time. She's lost in the ecstasy, I see her stomach trembling after only a few seconds. I wonder: how long has she been turned on for today? Does she think of things the way I do? Has she thought about fucking me at work, not able to focus? After a solid twenty minutes, and several smaller orgasms, we take a break.

"How did you know what to do? No guy has ever done that before." This is a sentence I will come to hear, over and over again.

"It just... came to me." I smile at her. I sit her up, and start fingering her again. This time, I'm really giving it to her. She starts to reach down to slow my hand down, which is moving like a jackhammer up into her swollen G-spot. Then she starts cumming, her pussy gushing out on to the couch, and she's looking around confused. After a solid minute of a deep, intense orgasm that leaves her confused, I say, "That's supposed to happen by the way—that's a deeper orgasm."

"Oh. Okay. That's never happened... I feel a little embarrassed."

"You squirted, that's supposed to happen."

"It is?"

"Yes, didn't it feel good?"

"I don't even know how to describe it... it was... amazing." She leaves, staggering and confused. The following days are filled with texts, overt flirting that doesn't even try to be clever or take advantage of innuendo. "I'll have to think about that one ;)" she says, when I demand to finger her asshole.

She was thinking about it all day, half-nervous I'm sure, but she was a Trinity girl after all. Thank God for those religious schools, for making debauched girls just wishing they could please their fathers. She starts talking about another guy she's been dating since the last time I was with her. She's plastered, and I'm amazed she made it here tonight. "He just didn't kiss me right. Nobody

16

kisses like you do." She's shoving her tongue in my mouth, and I return it as forcefully into her mouth. I throw her on to my bed and start fingering her, still exploring her mouth with my tongue during it. She's already lost in ecstasy, and her eyes are rolling back into her head. I'm getting a contact buzz off her cheap vodka. And for a second I think back to that big-titted nineteen year old Kiersten, who asked me in a flirty way to get her cake-flavored vodka for her and her friends, which I did. Cat's on her belly now, and her ass is red, as I guess I've been spanking it for some time now. The carnal nature of our encounters forces a fog over my mind, and I revert back to functioning on only the limbic level of the brain. I'm fingering her ass and pussy at the same time now, but something is unsettling about it. It could be that it slides in a little too easily, or the guttural moans coming out of her, or remembering her much more attractive friend that I wanted more, and I slowly lose interest. After she cums again, I leave her to lay

17

there, and I get up to wash my hands. I can sense a slight shame on her after I wash up, and we just lay there until she sobers up. She's got her arm around me, and I'm breathing heavily and sweating. She's wearing my gym shorts, her soft teenage breasts still out and she's smiling at me. My little TV off in the distance is playing Milo and Otis, the volume not loud enough to cover up her saying that she really likes me. "I really like you too, you should be with me." I say softer than her.

There are those of us who see gold in the eyes of our lovers, who patiently pursue and date with good intentions—babes that simply can't be anything other than head over heels. But what about the rest of us, the completely fucked ones with no hope, the drunks throwing up all night, the junkies shooting up, the aging beauty looking for just one last lay; the desperate ones who don't know how to take life any other way than all the way? How do we keep a relationship? She cares for me in her own way, and I want to care too, or at least admit that I do. But I had already distanced myself from her before even meeting her, convincing myself in my mind that she was only going to be a hookup. Maybe it's that Groucho Marx idea of not wanting to be a member of any club that would have me, or maybe it's the fear that what I really desire is a closeness that she's wanting to give me. She's texting me, begging me to hang out, and I'm put off simply by her wanting to be around me. She asks if she can call me. She starts telling me how she ended up sleeping with an Armenian guy at a club, and that she got herpes from him. "When was this?!" I snap.

"Don't worry. It was after we were together the last time."

"Well I mean, are you sure?"

"Yes."

"I'm... sorry that happened to you."

"It's not like you were serious about me anyway, and now you have a way out. I just want

19

to kill myself because no one will ever want me now."

"Hey that's not true, and that's not fair." I say, barely believing it myself. "Lots of guys would still want to be with you."

"But not you, right?" She cuts me off.

"I mean, I dunno. I haven't really been with many people. I'm like, not sure." I find myself kicking my gym shorts she was wearing off my bed, and taking off the sheets and blanket. "But don't say something like you're going to kill yourself. Lots of people have that, it's not really a big deal." And just like that, she is gone from my life— because I was too big of a pussy to just talk to her, to give her attention. In the following weeks, I find myself checking up on her, making sure she's still alive. She ends up getting serious with a musician, and moves into a house with him. I'm looking at her new Facebook pictures, and they have this glow about her that I never once saw when she was with me. She has happiness now. Some of us, however, will never recover: a parent that loses a child, a victim of rape, the broken ones. I don't want to think about her anymore, and the impulse to pick up my phone and check for casual sex dominates my thoughts...

Dana

Dana is a forty year old woman, that likes to say she is thirty-nine. Her genetics gave her the appearance of a twenty-five year old, except the subtle wrinkles in her face tell a story far more interesting than anything an actual twenty-five year old could ever tell. She pulls up in the shopping mall by my place, lost because my address shares a name with two other roads. She's in a Gremlin, a car that embodies everything about her—too old to start over again, and getting by as best as she could. She walks in to my trailer, her tongue already reaching inside my mouth. It's been years since she's been laid, as her husband was crippled in an accident at work and couldn't do anything other than talk and softly use his right hand, which was withered slightly. We texted in little windows, and she was excited to possibly squirt with someone. I tried to get her in to the idea of anal, but she had damage from giving birth to her son a few years earlier—before her husband was injured, and everything was okay in her world and she was just happy to be able to get pregnant so late in life. She's straddling me, and just the very act of mounting another person makes her moan with a small orgasm. My hands on her massive tits releases the start of a slow, building orgasm, one that's been pent up for years. She's laying down on my couch now, and I start roughly fingering her, and predictably, she's telling me to go gentler. She stops talking and starts screaming in delight as she starts gushing from her pussy.

"See? I told you. Do you want it again?" She shakes her head yes, and pulls me down hard with her hands into her mouth as I finger her again until she squirts over and over. This goes on for the next half hour until there's an actual giant puddle on my couch that seeps down onto the floor and in between the cushions. My clothes, which I throw on the ground, are getting drenched. She's sucking my cock now, and I keep telling myself in my head "I'm cumming," so that I can relax and release my cum into her mouth. She gets up, and goes to the bathroom to spit, and I act as if I don't notice. Now we're just sitting there, no bullshit anymore, both with undesirable small bellies that we just can't seem to get rid of, but unconscious to ourselves all the same. We talk for the next 20 minutes about TV shows and music, and about how so much of everything anymore lacks the feeling that draws people in. I wonder, for a brief moment while she's starting to put her clothes on, if this is all there is for me—that there are just other broken people that help you feel a little less broken for a few minutes, and then they're just gone from your life. I try to keep in touch with her, but she gets caught with someone else a few weeks in to it. I think too much about her child and husband and I feel shitty. A few more weeks of being more careful and we can maybe meet again, she says. I text her again after a few weeks and she asks, "who's this?"

Lexie

Somehow I luck into meeting Lexie, the
dreamiest of all manic pixie dream girls, and she
wants me. She texts me a picture of her ass, with a
My Little Pony tattoo tastefully done on it. I'm in
the projects, on night watch in an apartment
building. When I receive the picture, without
hesitation, I jerk off in the bathroom, and it's well
worth the paranoid twenty minute cleanup. I don't
hear back from her for a while, and I'm texting a
mutual friend about her, assuming it is simply over.
"That's a shame, you're a good guy and she really
needs that now. She's actually pregnant." I didn't
care—I would never care, not for her. In the past,
when a girl would bring up even the idea of getting
pregnant, I wouldn't be able to hide my fear, but
for Lexie, all I could think of was bettering myself.
Getting that new job I always imagined I would've
already had somehow, and providing and nurturing
for another person. I hear back from Lexie, she is
as concerned to have not heard back from me—

our texts were cancelled out by a passing storm. I'm excited that I've found out about her secret, and I want her even more. I think about her getting bigger, her nipples darkening and getting swollen, stretch marks appearing, late night cravings and mood swings, and even her fresh twenty year old face getting sallow with late nights and I want it all.

It's the next night and she's at my place. My giddiness is obvious, and I reek of complete desperation. Despite knowing that it's madness, I always approach these dream girls in the same way. They always know, somehow they always know, that I want them with every fiber of my being. We're talking and she's nervously laughing, because she knows what's coming. We've been flirting for days now, which is an epic poem anymore. She's saying that she has to go soon. "Well how about a kiss before you go?" We're kissing, and as I knew it would be, it's incredible. Her hair is soft, curls abound and perfectly done makeup, and all I can think of is how she did all this for me. She was thinking the whole time while getting ready about impressing me, resisting me, and having me. "That was nice, but... I was hoping to kiss you somewhere else."

"Oh yeah?"

"Mhm." She nods her head in approval, and she reveals from inside her sweater her plump, D-cup right breast with a perfectly pinkish-red nipple. She moans right as I take it in my mouth, and the ecstasy lasts only a few moments, but time still seems to slow down. There is a magic to us, to this meeting, even here in my unkempt chilly trailer, and we both feel it. But even still, I'm unable to live in the moment. I see beyond this rush, and I see only darkness. These moments—these moments of hands in hair, of shy giggles and perfumes and eyeliner and tongues hungering for each other, somehow always seem eclipsed... Maybe it is the fact that I don't have oil for my furnace as we huddle under the fleece blanket I had purchased that day, because I knew it would be chilly. Or maybe it's that my eyes can't hide much more than a thinly veiled secret, and the obviousness of my thoughts of fucking and marriage proposals showed in them. She's making some excuse about having to get up early, and I feel an ache inside me that wonders softly... Is this moment all there ever will be?

She's leaving, she has to go. "I miss you already! :D" I text a few hours later. And then there's her terrible response, telling me about the pregnancy, and that she feels like she deceived me. "No it's fine! Really, I think you're great! And... well, I already knew from our mutual friend." And from there it snowballs into she isn't ready for a relationship, that she thought she was, but she still needs to recover from being beaten by her ex, and yet there's still a part of her looking to find him again, to somehow take the blame. I don't want it to end, and I try, as always, much too hard to force it. In the days that follow, I'm recklessly driving around to various salons, where I know she works at one of them as a stylist, until I spot her blue Volkswagen to leave a love letter under her wiper blade, hoping this could somehow count as time together. That the days I spend contemplating slipping into drinking or worse could somehow, in some way, result in giving meaning to our short bond. That the days and weeks that followed stalking her on Facebook, and watching her relationship with another man, could somehow legitimize a sense of connection. That my keeping of the fleece blanket we huddled under that night, tucked up in my closet overlooking my bed and later in my car, at times just wrapping myself in it to try to live in that moment a little longer... That somehow this meant something, that we mattered. That I could be something more than a strange face in random dreams, her mind trying to file me away in her memories. And the darkness does come.

Grasping In the Dark

I'm at a convenience store, Gross's in Lewisberry, PA. One of those morally upstanding Christian boys, that is secretly a closet homosexual works there. He is nice enough: typical too lean of a frame, and overly tan complexion, with subtle feminine wrist flicks. I always wondered about him: Did he know? Would he ever know? Would he even live his whole life, end up getting married, never to even acknowledge that world—that his subconscious and his heart longed for? Or would it one day dawn on him, while going down on a stranger at a truck stop? The secrets we keep: the cocaine eyes returning from the bathroom, the defeated dreams and the unacknowledged soul-crushing enormities of reality, the fears, and even this clueless innocent. I love the attention from him—in fact, I even thrive on it. There is no real explanation for it either, as I'm not attracted to men. But it's the feeling of being overtly flirted with, desired, through body language, his eyes betraying him. Every once and a while, when visiting him, there are various teenage girls in yoga pants that I fantasize about following home, even forcing myself on their helpless selves. It's not something I want to do, and the self-disgust and shame at the thought always ends any pursuit. I would instead later, at home, picture them thumbing through phones, seeing something that reminded them of me, and secretly touching their nubile pussies. I would always half start to ask them out: "Gah, talking to you is so easy but it's always so busy in here." Always talking to them with a boyish charm and smirk. Every now and then they open up, talking about school and the boys they like that are ignoring them, and it's nothing but white noise, my eyes focused intently on their lips. Thinking if I was dating them, they would go their whole day talking to strangers, telling them about their petty lives, and wanting to end their day with me fucking their mouth, even slapping them in the face. And they would still look at me lovingly, even with gratitude.

I'm driving in Harrisburg when I see a homeless girl, white, somewhat dirty but actually pretty attractive. She's crying, really breaking down, and holding a sign that says "Ugly and homeless." I curse myself, that I don't have any money on me. I wonder if Fifty dollars would be enough for me to jerk off on to her face, maybe even try low-balling her at thirty. Then another thought enters my mind, of bringing her into my trailer, giving her ample soap and shampoos and conditioners, letting her shower. Offering her my bed, a meal, laying with her holding her as she weeps from joy, two desperate people finally finding someone to give all their love to. What if we could save each other? Both getting a chance to start new. I drive on by, "Ugly and homeless" circling through my thoughts the rest of the day.

I'm drawn back to Craigslist again. On average, I answer twenty ads an hour, even if at work. It's mostly submissives looking for a master or a daddy, or BBW's looking for a BBC. Most of them are disgusting, though some of them look halfway decent, but all of them are desperate. It's this desperation that truly satiates my lust. A MILF posting, wanting a three-way draws my attention.

"So would this be a two guys and you situation, or you, myself, and another girl?" I ask in response to her ad.

"I'm into everything. If it's two guys I'd want to watch you guys make out a little, and then give one of you guys head while the other fucks me. Or both of you fucking me. What are you into?"

"Oh you know, younger girls, pleasing and oral haha. :)"

"How young are we talking here? 11? 5?"

"What? No. God no, that's disgusting."

"Well you said younger and it doesn't matter to me, I know a girl that's 8 I could maybe get if you want."

"No, that's awful. I think I'm going to be sick. Don't message me anymore."

"Jeez I thought you said you were into younger girls. Do you still want to meet, and do you have any party favors?" I sink further into misery after talking to her, and after a while, I simply let go, and all at once it seems to come crashing down. The shit that we surround ourselves with, the distractions we have in between work and all the fucking and ugliness and faking of it all... And it crystallizes and I'm unable to remember the last time I was happy.

Gym Rituals

I'm strolling through GNC, checking my OkCupid profile. Only two visitors to my profile since I put up that picture of my back shot, dramatically lit in black and white. Only a few years old, with a waxed back, but still an accurate representation. The clerk is asking me if I need help finding anything, to which I shake my head no. One girl doesn't have any questions and answers on her profile, and only head shot pictures—a dead giveaway for a fat girl. I send her a "Hey" just for the attention, and when she responds with "Hi :)" I lose interest. I go up to the counter of GNC with a container of C4 pre-workout, relieved that they have the orange flavor, with a water. I start talking to the clerk, and ask him what his maxes are on the three big lifts, mostly to squash his numbers in conversation.

"Well I don't really go for maxes, I go more for tone and definition."

"What a fag." I say and start laughing as I'm opening my C4 and putting it in my water. "So yeah, I like definition too. There was this one product man, this Bitter orange stuff that worked amazing. But it has this synephrine stuff in it that works like ephedra I guess, and they were worried about it or some bullshit. It's like, anything that works they just recall."

"Yeah that's how it was with Jack 3D."

"Yeah! Exactly, and NO-Xplode. That shit worked. But yeah that Bitter Orange man, that and this Coleus Forskholli stuff. They had it standardized at like 14% at the Vitamin Shoppe by itself, but now everything is about the proprietary blend. And it's all about money—like, just put the stuff by itself. When I was on that man, I was a fucking animal!"

"Yeah man." He says, unimpressed.

"Well so what about the bench?"

"I really tend to just stick to dumbbells, for

more range of motion."

"Yeah I can do 325. Deadlift 580 easy." I'm saying, not really listening to him.

"Damn, that's impressive. I'd be too afraid of hurting my back."

"I feel it hitting me man, I gotta go get my pump on!" I start to leave, but instead keep talking about pull-ups versus chin-ups, and comparing the advantages of clean and presses versus incline bench presses. When he says that he uses the Smith machine, I leave in obvious disgust. I'm driving to the gym, checking my phone on the way, and hitting the refresh button on OkCupid to see if any new messages have shown up. I go to Pornhub.com at a red light and scroll through the thumbnails, and I click on a preview of a "cumpilation" outside my gym. I start watching gorgeous people debasing themselves for money, and I only want to see that climax of debasement. I switch to a compilation of women orgasming—

deep, intense, leg trembling orgasms. Even though I'm in the parking lot hard, my mind switches to gym mode. The beautiful girls turning in to complete whores, even if it isn't real, and the perfection of female orgasms is ample motivation for training. That end goal of being lean, attractive and, perhaps naïvely, hoping for a V-taper as well. That perhaps this, this would lead me to someone that truly wants me, who would love me, be interested in me. I just want to be desired.

There's still a few New Year's Resolution-ers floating around in the gym, some of them are really just taking up space for the time being. However, a few of them seem sincere, and I'm reassuring these few, and hoping to inspire confidence: "I was there too, I lost over a hundred pounds!" There's an older woman on the one machine that mimics an ab twist, and I flex my arms in front of her saying, "Hey baby, nope not flexing at *all*" while flashing a smile. She laughs and says "Uh-huh" and gives me one of those seductive looks with her eyes that says she's bound to be great in bed. Some tool that looks like he came out of a salt and pepper hair dye commercial comes up, and of course it's her husband. But I still stay there, flexing in front of her, doing chin-ups to really get my biceps rock hard. I lift up my sleeve to show the slight split between the biceps and triceps, with a simple bicep pose. She's glancing over, her piggy bank of a husband on an elliptical—clearly a joyless marriage. I'm asking her what her name is, and it sounds German, and I ask her if it is. She says "I've got a little German in me."

And I say "Would you like a little more German in you?" And she laughs, and I say "So when are we gonna hook up mamma?" Again, she gives me a seductive look and smiles.

"Oh you don't want me," she says and laughs, her eyes subtly looking me up and down, and it's obvious in her eyes she's picturing us fucking. There's another girl, this one in the weight room. Younger, probably 23, probably "really interested in nursing." She's wearing earbud headphones, music from an iPod or iPhone strapped to her arm, and she's poured into Spandex. I'm setting up my deadlift, and I bang out a few warmups of 135 pounds. 225 for two reps, 315 for two, 405 for one, all double overhand to further develop the grip. For the deadlift specifically, I find that warming up with too many reps takes away from my ability to do heavy sets. I then load up to 550 and do three reps, and I walk over to the younger blonde. "Hey did you check out that lift? How easy did that look?" I'm on the border of yelling to be heard over her headphones.

"Oh I'm sorry, I wasn't really paying attention." She says with a smile.

"Ah come on baby, I did that lift for you!"

"Ah, well it looks like a lot of weight. Do you compete?"

"You mean powerlifting?"

"Yeah, or bodybuilding."

40

"Nah, I can never get my ass to look good. What about you, what do you do for your butt? That's genetics, right?"

"Actually I didn't have that great of a butt to begin with, I just kept at it."

"Well whatever you're doing is working, because that ass is incredible."

"Thank you," she giggles and blushes, and says, "I try."

"Yeah so, next time I'm in here, we should workout together, get a sweat going." I say and wink unconsciously. "And you know, go out to dinner or *something*."

"Okay, sure." We both smile and I leave, wanting her to build up tension in her own mind about the coming days, hoping to bump into me.

Kristen

I'm driving at work at my second job, doing pizza delivery, when "Free Bird" by Lynyrd Skynyrd comes on the radio. I turn it all the way up, and during the climax of the song my hand is hitting the roof, and I'm reaching 60 mph coming around a sharp turn on a gravel road. I'm losing control and I try slowing down, but it's too late, and I'm accepting everything—that this is how I'll die, nothing accomplished and fucking around at work. I'm swerving left, almost flipping over the car on one side. I can't change... I can't change... Turning right, I go over a steep grass hill, only just barely missing a guard rail, the grass slightly wet, and I manage to do a 180 to get back on the road. I can hear my heart beating over "Free Bird", and I turn off the radio, calm myself, and go to the next delivery.

"Hey you!" It's Kristen, an older woman I started delivering to a few weeks ago. She's from New York, blonde and defeated. She opens the door, an invitation to come in as always. "How are you?" I'm so used to hearing "How much?" that I almost start to answer that question like an automaton, but I catch myself.

"It's, eh I'm doing okay I guess. What about you?"

"I'm so sore and tired from the fibromyalgia." She revealed this condition to me when I first met her.

"You know, my mom says that massages are the best thing for that." I'm relaxing her, letting her know subconsciously that I care about family, and I can provide for her.

"Oh I know, it's just I never have anyone to do it for me, and my husband is always working."

"Ah, well I'll give you one."

"You will?" She says with a look of hope in her eyes. I picture pizzas left half eaten and only bought to see me.

"Of course I will." She's on her couch, which looks like it cost more money than I make in a month. Her shoulders are slender, she's wearing a spaghetti strap tank top. She lets out a soft moan when I start rubbing, helpless to stop it. The oils of her skin mixing with the lotion on her back feels like some sort of heaven, and I picture her pussy, imagining her shaving it in the shower, making it hairless to feel young. I'm rubbing her anterior shoulders, and I feel her pain. The tendons tightly positioned in her arms—she carries herself like a person that holds everything inside. A dream she had was probably brought up, a vacation, or an idea about changing the furniture—anything for a "That's a great idea, honey, I love it" dopamine release response from her husband acknowledging her—when she's most likely met with "I'll think about it." Over time, she gets more and more whittled down, and I'm here rubbing her back, two strangers just needing to be close to someone. "I'm having a tough time reaching over the couch

44

cushion," I say, and she stands up. My hands are on the sides of her arms, moving over her fingers, back up to the extensor muscles of the forearm.

"Oh yess, that feels amazing." My hands naturally transition back to her sides, touching her lower back and hips. "Noo, not my love handles."

"Hush, you're beautiful." I whisper in her ear. She turns around, moving my hands over her sides. I'm tracing up and down her back, and I can hear her breathing heavily. I reach down and start rubbing the crest of her ass, and I can actually feel her have a small orgasm.

"Hey... careful now."

"What?" I say and give a charming smile. Her lips are hovering in front of mine, and my hands are running through her hair. I move to kiss her lips, but instead kiss her neck. Another small orgasm and she's trembling. She turns back around, not facing me, and takes my hands and moves them over her breasts and I squeeze them lightly. She's backing into me, and she moves her hand up the side of my face and knocks my hat off, and grabs my hair. She starts crying—something is wrong.

"Why did I get married? He's never here, and I moved here from New York to be with him. I'm about to turn forty... and it was now or never and he had money..." Every barrier down, she goes on. "I'm so old now, and it's like it never happened for me. I just need to go back to New York. Fuck him, he won't even notice... He thinks he can just leave me here and never talk to me. All I want is to talk to him."

"Shh, you're not old. You can talk to me." I'm giving her a hug, and she's writing down my phone number. When she texts me later in the week apologizing about everything, I ask her for a contact picture, and I never hear from her again.

Vanessa

I'm halfheartedly searching OkCupid again, when I come across an eighteen year old girl—short cropped hair, gauges, stoner. She has that look to her like she was a chubby girl, who never got over it emotionally, even after losing weight. Her lips are plump and still full of life, and she's not jaded about everything. "Hey, so I just want to say that you are absolutely adorable... and just, gah... I can't get over it. Anyway, I'm Sean :)"

"No you are the cute one!! :D You're a little bit out of my age range though," she says, I just turned 26, " but I might be willing to make an exception."

"Well if it makes your decision any easier, I love kissing, snuggling, giving massages, and I'm so warm like a furnace."

"I love all those things! Haha, we have a winner. And massages can lead to beautiful things happening." We're hurling each other at one another, both in love instantly.

"Oh really now? I should warn you, I'm an amazing kisser."

"Oh? We'll have to see about that. You know what? I say we just get rid of these things." She means our OkCupid accounts. "You're the one I want."

"I think... I think you're the one I want too." And in a haze, something happens with our limbic systems, and we're both impossibly drawn to each other. She gives me her number, then asks for my Facebook, and I'm dizzy that such a gorgeous young girl is interested in me. She likes several pictures of me on Facebook, and then sends a request to say that we're married. I go along with it, and then have to explain to my parents that it isn't a real marriage—but I wish it was, I think to myself after saying it. We meet for the first time at my place, only a few days later. She comes into my living room, wearing cutoff jean shorts and a T-shirt. The light scent of patchouli, as if she was wearing it and then showered, rises up off her. The pixie hippie, she's sporting an Alice in Wonderland tattoo on her left arm. I sit down, and without asking or saying anything, she straddles me. She places her head onto my chest, and we're holding each other. I breathe, and everything happens naturally with no rushing or trying too hard. Her lips are on mine, our eyes are closed, and we're lingering on each other's lips, everything we've ever experienced is being exchanged with this kiss. I open my eyes to see her eyes closed, her mouth slightly open. My hands move to the side of her head, leafing through her nymph hair. She takes off her shirt, and her pale C-cup breasts with barely noticeable stretch marks on them are revealed, and I love them. I love that a person has lived here, that this was a person that went through changes that I never knew to bring her here to me, and I love that she is letting me love her where no one else had cared to. Her eyes are still closed as I circle my tongue over her nipples, her bucking me. Her tiny fingers around my jaw, running through my balding hair without hesitation or acknowledgement of the hair loss. "I'm on my period," she says.

"It's okay." I say, as I'm taking her shorts off, pulling down her panties. I'm suckling her clit, giving her all my affection while doing it. She's warm, and strong tasting even though I'm careful to avoid licking inside her. She tastes good, distinctly her. She thinks too much about being on her period though, and so we spoon on my couch and watch *Fight Club*. We're only a little bit into the movie when she gets a text from her mom, and she has to go pick her up before work, but promises to come back tomorrow.

She's not even gone half an hour before she's messaging me on Facebook. "Ugh I really wish I wasn't at work on my period."

"Aw, I'm sorry honey. Hey, just think, you'll

be here wrapped in my arms tomorrow :)"

"^-^ I can't wait. I'm soo horny, it's torture!"

"Oh, well then I definitely shouldn't tell you about slowly sliding my cock inside your tight little pussy then, should I? :P"

"Ugggghhh stopp it! ;)"

"I am actually a little horny myself..."

"Do you want a picture of my boobs when my nipples were pierced?"

"No, I want you to get me off with your words... tell me what you'll do to me :)"

"Well... seeing that I'm on my period, maybe I'll just have to take your hard cock in my mouth? ;)"

"And, and you'll look up lovingly at me as my cum is filling your mouth? Won't you be a good girl and do that?"

"Anything for you, and I'll swallow."

"Okay, that did it! It's official, I don't want anyone else! Haha :)" A sentiment that no one else would have meant. It's the next day, nothing else matters and we burn so intensely that time itself seems to speed up to bring us back together. Her legs are spread, both our clothes still on, and I'm thrusting into her, my throbbing hard cock making her moan just by touching her mound. We're kissing, again obliterating planets with the intensity, we're making love even with clothes on there's just a soft magic to our entwined spirits. I want to penetrate her, for her to accept and take everything. I don't even mind her being on her period, but she does. I slide my fingers down her panties, rubbing her clit, plump and full of life. I start fingering inside her, not caring about the tampon, and I'm doing it in such a fast-arcing motion that I'm hitting her G-spot and clit at the same time. She's starting to cum, but some thought overrides it.

"I can't, I just am freaking out. I just

remember reading this horrible story about a girl getting a tampon stuck inside her, and I can't."

"It's okay... Well, you could always take care of me."

"I want to, I really do. I don't know, I just, my aunt who's really more of a mom than anything, well, she has cancer. And it's getting worse and I'm fighting with my best friend, and I don't think I can."

I see tears forming in her eyes. I remember the sincerity of teenage drama, and I'm going soft as my protective instincts take over. "Shh, it's okay. We'll just lie here, and when we wake up, I'll give you lots of kisses. I'll keep your aunt in my thoughts, and I'm sure your friend will come around."

"Okay, but I'm cold, do we have to have the AC on?"

"Trust me, when you wake up, you'll be thankful. Just snuggle up close to me and I'll keep you warm."

"Okay," she says with a smile. Her breasts, nipples now puffy from being under the blanket, are held in my hand. We both relax, we're both ourselves, and we don't have to fight to sleep. We both have dry mouths when we wake up. "Oh my god, I'm so fucking hot and I have to pee."

"I told you! I'm like a furnace!" And I let out a hearty laugh. There's something so beautiful in the way she traipses across the room, carefully stepping over clothes on the floor, her breasts swinging and her ass sticking out the sides of her panties. She's not a mastered and practiced painting, but a hurried sketch just rushing to get the idea down, almost as if she'll always be moving too fast to be perfectly captured. She's getting dressed, and I'm just enjoying watching her. The ease of her putting her bra on, something that is a joyful struggle in foreplay done so matter-of-factly and efficiently—she starts to slide on her tank top. "No," I say, "leave it here. When I get sad and miss

you too much, I want to be able to breathe you in."
She smiles, and says she wants a cigarette before
leaving, afraid her mom will smell it if she smokes
in her car. While she's outside I'm taking a piss,
thinking about our fingers interlocking just hours
earlier, her clenching so tight.

She's on my lap again, seeming down that
she has to go. "All I want all day is this," I'm saying,
"to come home to an adorable girl and have her sit
on my lap and tell me about her day, and to be able
to play with her hair."

"I want to go to California. And to study
botany."

"Botany? Plants?"

"Mhm," she says and nods her head.

"Don't go to California, not yet anyway.
Stay with me for a little while, and then you can go.
I won't hold you back from leaving, I just want to
soak up as much of you as I can before you go."
We're exchanging more soft, lingering kisses, and

every terrible memory fades into obscurity.

"I have to go to work," she says with eyes closed, "and Jackie and I made up, it was a stupid fight that was complete bullshit."

"Oh? What about?"

"Ugh it's too much to get into. I have to go, I'll text you later."

"I'll miss you, here lemme get another smooch before you go!" She smirks, walks back over, and I'm grabbing her ass while we're kissing.

"Bye," she says, sweetly. Two hours pass, and I'm reading a message from her on Facebook. "I don't think this is going to work out. I just feel like we'll run out of things to talk about. :(" I'm trying to tell her about destiny, that everything that has happened in our lives was all building to this attraction between us, every struggle and triumph, drawing us nearer to one another. I'm telling her I have so much love to give, that it's a planet and that it's just too much to be contained within one

56

person. "I'm sorry :/" she says. And really, what can I tell another person? About the old-time strongmen? About how ice was cut off the Susquehanna in the winters, and insulated in sawdust, and that it was a major export? That we are in essence amino acids being broken down over and over? That Lincoln once whispered to his wife Mary Todd, "They're only children for so long," when she was upset over their offspring' rambunctiousness? Or did I dream that part of history... But what she really means by things to talk about is getting high on ecstasy at raves, dropping acid and having sex, and getting stoned and laughing at bad movies on Netflix. I hold her shirt I asked her to leave behind, smelling it, taking it all in as I try to make myself cry harder than what I am. The Wellbutrin makes it easier to move on, as if her memory is only a bruise—it hurts to the touch, but when left alone, it's forgotten.

Things That Can't Be Taken Back

There's a cool crispness in the air, the seasons are changing from fall into winter. I'm at work at Security, my sister en route, bringing me leftover deviled eggs from a party of hers. I'm messaging girls on OkCupid again waiting for her, a blonde finally got back to me that's into anal and gave me her number. "Hmm yeah you can come over, but I'll have to sneak you in."

"Wait, you live at home?" She's twenty-four years old. "Would you be able to come to my place instead?"

"Yea lol I'm at home, for now. And no I can't go to your place. There is one other thing too..."

Oh no, a catfish I think, but say "What is it?? Haha :)"

"Well, I'm not the biggest fan of your facial hair, do you think you could shave it? For me?"

"I hate my face clean shaven, but I would

consider it."

"I'll make it worth your while ;)"

"Done."

"And your chest hair?"

"Ugh no, it itches way too badly when it grows back in. I only shaved it once for these bodybuilding progress pictures. Never again!"

"Pleeeasssee" she says, and texts me a picture of her lips pursed like she's about to cry. "I'll do anything you want."

"Anal? And I want to cum in your mouth."

"Well, anal isn't too bad, and sure that's fine. But only if you shave." I'm turned off by her ultimatum, and the thought that she thinks pussy, or in this case ass, can get her anything she wants. I'm thankful that my sister has arrived and I'm not alone anymore.

"Hey brother" she says, "here are the eggs. Nobody wanted them for some reason."

"Really? I think they're *sin*fully delicious."

She looks around, noticing the light dusting of snow starting to flurry, and for some reason, this seems like the right time for her to drop a bomb on me. "So I'm pregnant." She says with a smile.

"Take *care* of it" I say in a way that she knows means abortion. It is these words and my tone, the shy and hidden look of hurt on her face, the subtle wince she gives, that I'll think of as I'll hold him later as an infant. A quiet, warm body in my arms, just aching for love and attention. I think about how, growing up children will mark their height in a home, parent-teacher conferences, buying sports equipment, guitars, all the interests we try to develop, helping a person that came from you... and I realize that will always seem out of reach for me. That kind of money and having my life together just feels impossible right now, and I'm afraid of how much I actually want it.

"Well I'm happy about it, and I really hoped

that you would be happy for me too."

"I'm sorry" is what I wish I say, but instead I say, "meh whatever." My cells continue to divide over and over again, continuing my life. My sperm rise and daily swim into nothingness. My heart beats to pass on my genetic material to someone— all for nothing. I start to think about that hippie chick with three kids. "I'm still lactating ;)" she said, and she wanted to get stoned and have me fist her endlessly. I send her a message while my sister is still there: "I just got to thinking about you, and your lovely breasts needing milked, and your pussy needing adored and just had to say hello :)" I am regretting blowing off that blonde Tara, and send another feeler message saying that I would shave my chest, but it was too half-hearted and too late, much like my eventual apology to my sister.

Liebling

Amidst all the mediocrity of online dating—
the bipolar messes who quote Marilyn Monroe in
their profiles, and anthems of not looking for
hookups while always starting sex talk first, twenty-
one year olds with three kids that are a package
deal (beggars can't be choosers isn't in their
vocabulary), girls claiming to wait until marriage
who are only one night of shots and getting felt up
away from fucking in a club—is a darling. She's
nineteen years old, a sarcastic blonde but not an
overly confident one, we both have a dog named
Max, and she's part German. She likes to speak
German with her sister sometimes, only in a
perfunctory way—but it still makes her more
mysterious and interesting. I ask her if she has any
goddamned clue how beautiful she is. She could
be a doppelgänger for Margot Robbie, only
somehow softer in her features and realness. She's
like something straight out of a Renaissance

painting: Creamy ivory skin with cheeks that have just the subtlest hint of rosy hues, eyes as deep and blue as Caribbean waters, supple D-cup breasts and hips to match, and a smile that could make a man do anything. She is simply too beautiful to be on OkCupid. She is the kind of woman who has to see messages all day from horny old slobs, and while some days she likes it, other days it wears her down. I understand how a person can both be hypersexual, and be sex repulsed at the same time. I tell her that when I look at her, I think we both should stop giving the best of ourselves to the worst people. I tell her that the stars were here a millennia before us, that their burning has been going on for an eternity, always drawing us together. I tell her that the only explanation for anything is that everything is destined—we can't change the past, and our presents are all bringing us together in the only way it could have been. I'm trying to say that every person you encounter, including the unsavory ones, is bringing you to the next meaningful person. That it is indeed all the low points of our lives, that we don't have a say in, that bring us to all the highs. I'm able to tell her these things with such ease through messages, but I know that I'll be too awestruck in person to be able to articulate these deep thoughts. I tell her that she is nothing short of a dream, and that I want nothing more than to kiss her endlessly, and to massage her shoulders while kissing her neck, and to lick up and down her wonderful thighs and kiss my way to her pussy, to give her more pleasure than she can handle and suckle her clit until she can't take it anymore, and that we'll snuggle up together and have sleepy conversations until we pass out in each other's arms.

I'm towards the end of a miserable 24-hour work day. Already having worked five hours at the pizza shop, I agreed to pick up an extra shift at security for a total of 19 hours at security as well. "Hey, I'll have the house to myself tonight if you wanted to hangout ;)" She, Taylor, texts me, and my heart skips a beat.

"Baby, are there any other days you would be free?"

"Well, it's just that my mom and her boyfriend and my sister are all out at a movie. It could be a while before that happens again."

"It's just, you gotta understand, I've just been working so long. Mmmaybe if I had a picture tease I would think about it :)"

"If you're coming over or not, it's fine with me. Either way I'm getting in the shower now." She attaches a picture of herself with her ass facing the mirror. She is somehow able to snap a picture looking casual, no blur—there's just a hint of a lip, and an onion booty that makes you cry to look at it.

"Holy shit! You know what, fuck it, I'm coming over. :) There's just one thing though. I am very tired. And as much as I want to do more, I don't know if the little guy can. So is it okay if... it's just about you tonight?"

"Well, I would really like that :) But I also love to give, and will want to try anyway. ;)"

"I'm just very shy, when it comes to my own body. I just don't want your feelings to be hurt if nothing happens."

"They won't be, and there's no pressure at all."

"Will an hour from now be too late?" I'm half an hour away from my shift being over, and the fastest shower and drive of my life away from getting there.

"Nope, see you then ;)" I'm barreling down the highway, and somehow my senses are heightened to the point where I can see miles ahead with ease. I'm too much of an optimist to think of her as a catfish, and my skin starts to peel tightly around my eyes as my hands become sweaty. I get lost right as I'm nearing her place, and I pull off to the side of a backroad to take a piss. I pretend that I'm talking to someone on the phone as a car passes. I finally make the right turn, all of this building tension in me is exhilarating. I see her there, on her porch steps in a hoodie and basketball shorts, as if this was no big deal to her. But I'm nearly trembling, a man that caught feelings too soon, and who's thinking about a long-term relationship filled with anniversary dinners and trips to planetariums to learn more about the stars that she so loves. "I heard this big diesel truck pull down my road—I thought it was you and I got really turned on." She says, showing all at once her tomboy side who never really felt pretty, so she got to know all the ins and outs of cars. Who worked on trucks with her dad, and who knows infinitely more about them than I do, and who posts memes making fun of cars like my Ford Focus. "The stars are so beautiful tonight."

"Yeah, they are. Not as beautiful as you though." I flash a genuine smile, and I'm completely sincere in my cliché words. How would I begin to say we don't even know how big the

Milky Way galaxy is? I sit down next to her, she's smoking a bowl.

"Do you mind if I finish this?" She smiles, her golden hair is filtering out of her hoodie, being illuminated by the light of the stars and moon. I try to tell her that the moon's light is only a reflection of the sun, much like the only good in me is only brought out by her. But I'm instead rubbing her ass and kissing her neck.

"Go ahead and finish, I don't mind," I whisper.

"I'm surprised you haven't sung 'oh my darlin', oh my darlin' Clementine'."

"What do you mean? Oh duh, because of your last name." I chuckle and say, "After hearing a lifetime of 'Houston we have a problem,' I'm a little understanding about last name sensitivity."

"Do you want any of this? I feel bad for smoking in front of you."

"Nah, you go ahead." I say as I start caressing her back.

"Mmmmm, you are making it very hard for me to concentrate." I slide my hand down her shorts, to feel a supple and perfect ass. It's all real and really happening. This completely wonderful, and gorgeous stoner girl is here in my hands and I couldn't be happier. "Let's go inside," she says with a smile. The TV is on, and I catch a flash of her Netflix queue. Courage the Cowardly Dog, Metalocalypse, Edward Scissorhands, and on her table is a DVD case of Donnie Darko from the library. I dedicate it all to memory. She's showing me around, but she leads me back to her room quickly. Her walls have posters on the walls of various bands I don't recognize, except for Insane Clown Posse—which have a reputation of not being the best band, but I like her even more for liking them. I admire her ability to openly like what she likes. Somehow this person went unnoticed her entire life, inexplicably. There are parts to her, like

70

myself, that seem contradictory, and I want to discover them all. We both are a little slutty, but neither of us really want to be, it's just how we were made.

I take my shirt off, "I told you I was really hairy," and I laugh and take my pants off too, but leave my boxer briefs on.

"I like it—you're my beast." She says, and I'm bending down, kissing her as she's on her bed. I take her shorts off, and I know this turns her on, as she made it very clear that she likes dominance. I'm rubbing my hand over her panties, telling her to take her shirt off. She does, and her nipples are so hard that they're poking through her bra. I take it off with ease, as I'm kissing her, our tongues rolling over each other with nothing held back, no pecks or awkward one-mouth-open one-mouth-closed kisses. I'm kissing my way down her neck to her breasts, cupping them as I start to lick them. From her reaction of a near orgasm, I see her entire sex life. Getting fucked from behind hard for five minutes, or pounded missionary-style while her breasts are being grabbed hard, and her being left there after the guy gets off. My fingers are sliding up and down her clit, she moans softly. I pull her panties down, to reveal a perfectly shaved and shaped pussy, with a scent rising into the air that turns me carnal. I start fingering her G-spot while kissing her, and I'm making her bed wet with her cum. When I put my free hand on her hip, and really give her a good man handling, she squirts all over me and herself.

"Holy shit," she says, "I didn't think I could squirt... How did you do that?"

"These hands were just made for you, I suppose." I say, "Do you want more?"

"Yes please." Over the next half hour, I give her forty G-spot orgasms, and when my forearm is too tired, I start to give her oral sex. She tastes strong, like she recently had her period, or is about to start. I lay there, suckling away on her clit and feel the release of dopamine in my brain with each orgasm she has. It's better than my own orgasm, I have so fetishized the female orgasm. We're lying there, exhausted, my forearms filled with blood and swollen to the point that I can't move them. "I... How did you? ... I've never had... an orgasm with a man before..."

"Shh, that's okay."

"I, I really want to suck your cock now."

"I don't know if I could even handle it..." My forearms are too pumped, nearly all of my blood is within them, and I don't think that I can get hard. "I'm very shy about myself."

"Well that's okay, I haven't been with many guys. Can I try at least?"

"Okay," I say, and I slide down my boxers, trying to hold back my excitement. I see beautiful women walking down the street, talking to people about their day, and they look so well-maintained and dignified, and underneath it all can be a woman who's cock hungry. It's this psychological switch from being well-mannered to sexually powerful creatures that turns me on. She's sucking, and she's actually amazing, the eye contact makes it so intimate. I'm half hard, as my blood is too pooled in my forearms, coupled with poor circulation. "Jerk me off and kiss me," I say, and she starts stroking while kissing me. After a while, I feel bad, and I tell her it isn't going to happen. I kick myself for not getting the blowjob first, I never learned to leave anything for myself. "I'm sorry, it's not you. Really. I really like you, and I think you're gorgeous. I just, well, this is kind of tough to say. I've been on this anti-depressant, and it's been giving me problems... sexually. I've never had a reason to get it checked out before... I've never had a girl that I cared so much about, to talk about it with, because it's embarrassing..."

"But now you do?" She says, with a smile that could move me to climb a mountain, to topple buildings, to do anything for her.

74

"Yes..." I say, with near exhaustion at the release of the weight on my chest from carrying that around. "Hey, how about that massage?"

"Okay," and she sits up in front of me. I'm rubbing her shoulders to many pops and cracks.

"What's that from?"

"From when I played sports, lacrosse and stuff."

"Aww, poor thing." And I'm rubbing her beautiful breasts again, turning her neck around to kiss her. "Sorry, I got distracted."

"It's okay," she says, and I'm fingering her again. Even in this mechanically disadvantaged position, I make her cum with ease. "Oh my god, my bed is soaked!" We both laugh. She wants me to make a video of her orgasm, and even though I can barely move, I do. She squirts everywhere, as my hands are simply too powerful for her to resist. We're laying on the bed, and I'm next to this goddess, both of us fully drained. Her ass is slightly poking out from the covers, and I look over to see a picture of her in glasses on her nightstand, and what I feel between these two moments is not lust at her naked body. Sometimes fucking is the goal in dating, but it is *this* real nakedness that should be the goal. That this same person who is here in this picture with a goofy grin, is now naked beside me quietly looking at her phone... And she is just existing and allowing me to see her existing, that she is a person. That like myself, is weak at times and capable of crumbling, she is horny at other times, she's sick in bed other times, that she's weighing decisions on hair products, and will pursue jobs and love like anyone. We're all imperfect, trying to survive and understand life, and I'm here catching a glimpse of her because we're both spiritually naked, and comfortable. And it's so obvious, that I love her. It's as if there has always been a magnet inside me, beating within my chest as an unconscious compass, always drawing me to her and that another magnet, cast in the same mold, also exists within her. And every touch and kiss has been divine, because a part of myself has existed in the universe within her, and it is right here in front of me now. We try as people to cover up the enormity of such a thought with random sex, social media updates, with eating junk food and working ourselves to death, because such a profound truth—that another part of you is out there—is simply too big.

We lay there for a few minutes. "I would stay if you like."

"I think I would like that." she says. "Ugh, but my sister is on her way home. She just started driving recently. I really need to get my own place. She'll try to use you being here as a way of getting me in trouble with my mom." I'm so grateful to live alone, despite the fact it's an older, draftier trailer—I'm free.

"I understand. We can hang out next week, maybe?"

"Um, we'll see. I definitely want to, I just don't know if I'll have the house to myself again. Oh yeah, let me show you something!"

I'm pulling my pants on, and I accidently step on her laptop. She's a messy person like myself. We're all messes, just in hidden ways. "Just step on my computer, why don't you," she says with a cute sarcastic tone. She shows me to her sister's room, and she brings me out a shirt that has a picture of a pug on it.

"Oh my gosh it's perfect! Just like my Maximus."

"I know! My Max lives with my dad."

"That's adorable!" I say, genuinely excited. "I'd like to one day be able to be in bed with you and all the dogs cuddled up." We're kissing more, and I'm caressing her. Right at my fingertips could be the love of my life, explosions happen softly in my heart and I'm trembling unnoticed. It finally comes time for me to leave, but I soak up every

78

possible second of holding her before I do. Later, I'm falling asleep happy: Wonderfully fading, intense, manic happiness. This feeling, I would walk through hell and back, endure a lifetime of purgatory, crawl over glass—if only it meant that I could keep this feeling longer.

On the Tip of My Tongue

A few weeks of texting back and forth turns from October to November, species dying off or hibernating, an entire world existing outside of Taylor and I simply don't care. I send her cute socks, which she told me is her favorite gift, in the time that we can't be together. "You're perfect" she says, when she receives them. I'm pressing to see her again, and she has the house to herself this weekend. She's at work on a Friday morning, and I'm sure that her entire week has been building to our meeting. I tease her at work with sexts, and I want to test her limits.

"I want you sitting on that beautiful peach all day thinking about my tongue as deep in your pussy as it can go, only being taken out to lick up and down your ass."

"Unggh you're torturing me :P"

"Aw I'm sorry honey, did I make you soak through your panties?"

80

"Yes, jerk ;)" I end up calling off work, not wanting any interruptions to my night. I am so blinded by lust and love. We never question why we're in love, we just allow ourselves to be staggeringly consumed by it. Is she good looking, and do other people find her beautiful? Yes. Are there chemical reactions happening inside my mind even at the thought of her, undressing her, hearing her soft moans as I kiss the crest of her hips? Yes. But she is also so new, filled with so many possibilities. My thoughts are racing with the possibility of telling her that I love her, and of buying a home together... Always so many steps ahead of where I actually am.

I show up at her place, after taking a rip-off Cialis from a friend. It's only a half dose, and it's giving me a pump. She shows up at the door, and already we're both flush. I'm kissing her hard, and squeezing her breasts over her black bra, leaning her back onto the couch. Her clothes are lost in the fray, and I can't discern if I've actually taken the

81

time to take her clothes off, or if I've just ripped them off. I spend a long time suckling her nipples, getting lost in the act and transforming into a creature dependent on them, as if they have my very life force within them. I take my tongue and drag it down her immaculate body, down her hip to a similar location that is extremely ticklish on myself. There's some sexual nerve buried here, and she's trembling so hard that her feet are thumping on the floor. I allow this tension to build for several minutes, this bodily buildup of an orgasm, before yanking her panties down. Her pussy looks somehow softer than I remember, the scent is lighter (which isn't necessarily a good or bad thing), and I envelop her entire pussy with my lips. Each drop of precious fluid is savored, each lip caressed and tongued, and her throbbing clit is satisfied. "Let's go to your bedroom." I say, and I follow her there. She lies on her back, I take my hands and gently spread her legs, two fingers sliding into her with ease. Within a matter of seconds, she is having a series of squirting orgasms.

"How do you do that? You just, you know exactly where to go..."

"I already told you—these hands were made for you." I smile at her, and torture her with 20 minutes of nonstop orgasms. But it's no longer enough, and I command her to "get on all fours for me." She complies, putting her ass in the air, and as I start licking her lips again, I put just a little bit of my finger in her ass, not wanting to go too deep too soon. There isn't resistance, so I go deeper still, and it tightens involuntarily on me. This of course is all foreplay, as what I really want is to lick my way to that heavenly release I feel of giving pleasure, the actual physiological release in my body that is better than an orgasm when I make a girl cum. I start licking around her ass, inching my way closer to her asshole, needing to taste it, and she starts trembling even harder when my tongue goes inside her tight asshole. There's no poetry—it tastes the only way an ass can—and I love it all the

83

same. She's positioned in such a way that I can also finger her pussy, thrusting right into her G-spot. "You like that? Me licking your ass?"

"Mhm," she moans, and I tell her to rub her clit. I spread her ass and get my tongue inside her as deep as it will go, and even though she doesn't squirt her orgasm is actually more intense, and as a result, so is my pleasure. It feels like I came in my boxers, without actually touching myself. I roll her back on to her back, and I want to gently lie on her and penetrate her. Something is off, and as I make this move her legs start to close, and I'm not just imagining it either. I brush it off, too exhausted to care, and I want it to happen when she wants it to. "My sister is going to be home soon. I'm sorry, I really want you to stay the night," she offers as a reason for stopping things tonight.

"It's okay," I say, supportively. "Here, let me get my stuff ready, and we'll just relax on your couch."

"Okay!" She says, excitedly, with a smile.

She's wearing a hoodie with her hair tucked underneath, but it's flowing out. "I really like you, you know?"

"I know" she says, and I kiss her on her lips, both of us hovering on the other's lips longer than most would.

"Don't you just hate that when people give just pecks for kisses? But not you—you're the best kisser." And we kiss some more.

"You're not too bad yourself," she says, eyes closed with a half-smile. She's sitting on my lap, our bodies warming each other, and she says reluctantly, "my sister will be home soon," in a whisper in my ear with a softness only a girl can have. "We only have 15 minutes".

"I know," I say, and greedily take another kiss. "These lips are yours, and these hands. These hands were made for you. They're your gift." Sitting here with her is the same for me as standing before art—how it changes you without you knowing it. And the time passes, in the way it passes when you look at the ocean's waves breaking against the coast on a beautiful day. It goes by quickly because it's so serene you lose track of it. "I'm so into you" I say.

"I know," she whispers, so quiet you can hear her heartbeat underneath the words. In our own ways, neither one of us has ever really been equipped with the skillset to know what to do when you fall in love.

"And you don't mind if I text you too much and I'm a little obsessed?"

"Not at all" she says, and smiles. If I could have one moment, where I could stay forever, it would be here. If that flash of the moments of life that stretches into eternity turns out to be true—I would be completely fine existing only here. I drive home, brimming with so much dopamine that it feels like it's seeping out of my pores.

Christmas

Her responses are trailing off a bit, but she responds to a majority of the sexual texts that I send her. "I love watching you cum" I say, after she e-mails me a short video of me getting her off. "I'm going to fuck you next time ;)"

"Mmm yes please, and let me suck your cock."

"You want my dick baby?"

"Yes baby, please." When I'm trying to make definitive plans over text, I don't hear back from her. I'm texting a few other girls, to avoid smothering her. "Cushions" I call them to my boss, just in case she ends up rejecting me, I have some comfort in girls who I'm not serious about to soften the blow. Christmas is approaching, I'm looking forward to the $200.00 my stepdad gives me every year, still trying to pay for all the times that he scared the shit out of me. Hands against the wall, hitting me with a 2x4 for not helping lay down laminate in the kitchen; saying "go ahead call the fucking cops" after slapping my teenage face. But it's more than the money. I can't explain it, but somehow, the need grew to love and forgive him. I'm maxing out my credit cards to splurge on Taylor, and can use the money. I have also been working on a couple creative projects: A drawing of Jack Skellington, a recording I did of me singing with a friend the German cover of "I Want to Hold Your Hand" ("Komm, gib mir deine Hand"), a framed picture of my dog Max, and a long handwritten note about how incredible it is that our paths intersected. I'm on the phone arguing with a company that specializes in socks, Sock It to Me, to see why my online order for Taylor isn't going through. "Now listen to me, I *need* these socks man. And I don't care what the shipping cost is." I also include a cute stuffed animal for her, and remember that she likes Reese's Peanut Butter Cups. They make these half pound cups around the holidays, and I buy her one. I text her a picture of me holding it while making a goofy face.

"I want it, and you to snuggle while I nibble on the crinkly edges of that giant cup of heaven."

"That is maybe the single greatest thing anyone has ever said to me." I'm texting her later that night, trying to get a lock on when I can see her again. A few days pass without a reply. I don't like her not responding, and I go on her Facebook to look at the guys she's friends with. My restlessness isn't fading, and I try working it off by going to the gym, but my mind is too wired, and tears are starting to form in my eyes. I see a guy next to me doing light dumbbell work, and I recognize him. There was a girl I used to be in love with, and he was her boyfriend briefly. I load a barbell up to 575 pounds next to him, and rip out eight vicious reps on the deadlift, and I shout out "that's fucking right! Fuck you pussy!" While looking right at him. He's the brother of a gym rat friend of mine, and we all laugh it off. After lifting I'm standing in the bathroom, on the verge of hyperventilating from too many thoughts choking me. I'm leaving the gym with tears in my eyes at the thought of Taylor with someone else.

A few more days pass, and I finally hear from her. "Honey I'm sorry, I can't do anything tonight. I'm in the hospital."

"What? What happened?!"

"Me and my mom were hit by a drunk driver earlier in the week."

I think back to how anxious I was when I didn't hear from her. "Why didn't you... tell me earlier?"

"I'm sorry, I didn't think about it. I've just been in so much pain."

"I know I was being selfish. I feel like such an idiot now. I do have these gifts for you, that I think will really make you feel better!"

"I don't know if I'm up for gifts right now. My mom and dad are fighting on the way home and I have a goddamn headache." I feel my panic attack worsening. My entire body is trembling, my skin is breaking on the backside of my hands from gripping the steering wheel so tightly. I'm already on the way to her house, unable to soothe my anxiety. I text her while driving, asking if it would be okay if I drop off her gifts. I stop at a diner by her house, wanting to calm down after driving in case I get to see her. I'm telling her how much I like the food at the diner. "Ew are you sure? Haha, I think that place is terrible."

"Well yeah, I don't know I must've just been really hungry haha." She's back to not responding to my texts on the way there, and I think about how sometimes our phones just don't like interacting. iPhones have difficulty accepting non iPhone messages sometimes, converting them from iMessage to SMS text message, I tell myself. I reflexively take a Wellbutrin to try and calm myself. When I arrive at her door, I'm texting her that I'm there but she's not responding, and even though

10 minutes go by I still stand there a little longer. I finally leave the package of gifts on her doorstep, knowing that this would be the only thing that could calm me down. How many times have I done this same thing, only to have it fail? It doesn't really matter, because all I care about is giving... give enough and maybe they'll love me like I love them.

"Honey, my mom plopped two soaking boxes on my bed this morning." She texts me the next day.

"I'm sorry :(I didn't know it was going to rain!"

"Boo... I'm killing you the next time I see you for not waiting to give these in person. Do you have any days off this week, maybe this weekend? I wanna get a hotel room with you and have you unwrap your ace bandaged wrapped gift (AKA me), as long as you're gentle <3 It's taking a lot for me to get around at work today, my partner in crime isn't here today, but I don't have a Staples supply order coming in, so I don't gotta worry about lifting anything. And man, I really wanna go to the gym— but oh well. Text me when you wake up honey, I'm crushing galaxies with every step today, by the way." She's wearing the constellation socks I got her... So much joy is flooding my senses with her text, that I think I might be having a heart attack. Finally... it finally happened. I found a girl that will let me give her endless pleasure, and spoil her with gifts just for the sake of spoiling.

"I'm sorry I didn't wait, you just seemed so sad yesterday. And like, I already had it all together, and I thought you were mad at me when I didn't hear from you. I've dealt with a lot of shit girls you know, so my brain gets retarded haha. I tend to always have slam dunk gifts by the way, you're just the lucky one in my cross hairs this year :) The one thing I wanted to do more than anything was make a painting of you riding a unicorn with Toki Wartooth, but I kept fucking up and gave up in frustration. It took me a second to get what you were saying about galaxies lol!" "Lol" is a texting phrase that I don't usually use, but I pepper it in conversations with Taylor because she uses it, and I'm mirroring her habits for likeability. "I know how much you love the stars, and I figured that this way when you look at your socks you can contemplate your future, and how awesome your socks are haha. I told the woman at the sock company, 'if the gifts go well this year, lady I'm putting your kids through college,' lol."

"When's your next day off?"

"I have a bunch haha. I work today and Saturday only this week, the way the holiday fell. I might be able to get off earlier Saturday night, but it could be tricky."

"So like... Are you going anywhere for the holidays?"

"Nope, just to my parents' house earlier in the day. You really want me now don't you? :)"

"Yes, I do. When is a good day for you?"

"Thursday, Friday, Sunday. Let's just live on each other the whole time. Even Christmas night could work. Maybe Friday is best, because then you have the night off, and we can stay the night. I wish it was now, I really want to finger you and lick and suck on your tongue, morning horniness lol." I can't even go a few texts without reminding her of my sexual prowess, because I want her to desire me, and I'm afraid of her viewing me as a friend.

"That works for me :)" And I go into Christmas with a vigor, knowing that I'm going to have a weekend of crazy hotel sex, cumming all over her face multiple times, groping and caressing her in the shower, complaints being called in as I thrust into her and take her from behind while she's pounding up against the headboard, and waking up an hour before checkout and fucking her mouth under the covers, making her gush all over the comforter. The staff will smell her and me and the sex in the room—it will saturate the air and permeate the walls and filter out underneath the door and everyone will know something carnal and wonderful happened. Maybe then I can tell her how I really feel... that when I'm near her there are swelling symphonies within me. Maybe I don't even need these things anymore as a pretense...

A few days go by. I'm at home with family and I playfully put on a Santa hat, while Max, my pug, is wearing elf ears. I have my picture taken and send it to Taylor, saying "Merry Christmas! :)" in the text. A few hours pass until she responds.

"I'm not having a good night."

"Oh no, what's wrong?" But she doesn't respond, so I send a couple more pictures of Max and me, clueless that I really need to just leave her alone to show her I don't need to know her, and be mysterious... These are things I was never taught to do when you have feelings for someone. "Well muffin, I know you are in pain, so I hoped cute pictures of Max would make you feel better. I'll talk to you later darling, try to feel better :D" I write, too available and too sincere.

More days pass. The hotel never happens, and my texts become more desperate. To dilute the desperation, I go back to messaging people on OkCupid again, preparing to soften the inevitable blow with (hopefully) a blowjob. I find an older married woman, who wants me to "kidnap" her husband. This is supposedly some role play involving breaking in wearing a mask, hogtying him, and leaving him there while I fuck his wife in another room. Apparently they both get off on it, and even I'm a little into the idea. I tell her that I want to fuck her, and make her swallow every drop of cum I give her, and she's fine with everything. "Whatever you want to do to me, I will suck your cock, beg you to fuck me in the ass. Just please come in and tie him up and berate him, maybe hit him a few times with a baseball bat. He wants it, it's consensual." She keeps begging me to come over. There's something wrong, though, and it's not just the paranoid feeling I have floating around in my head that this all could be a setup of sort... There's a feeling of guilt. We've never defined what we are exactly—whether or not I was Taylor's boyfriend. It never seemed like a conversation to bring up, because I didn't want to scare her off by talking about it too early. And I start thinking more about her tender body, bruised after that car accident, and her tiny heart being crumpled up by the world. I like the idea of being her man, and belonging to her alone. I decide that even if I'm not going to hear from her for days, whether with her or without her, in whatever limbo I am in, that I will endure it without the crutch of balancing out my need for attention with other people.

Date With Destiny

"Honey, if you're awake, I'm about to get off of work and go to York for some shopping. I can't do the hotel thing tonight. I gotta take my mom for her colonoscopy tomorrow morning. And... Did you send me flowers?" At last it's Taylor again, my love! It slipped my mind that I did order her flowers online a few days ago, when I was feeling especially devastated at the thought of her still hurting from the accident.

"Yes I did :) What are you shopping for?"

":) I have to get a new phone, I was thinking Best Buy."

"Okay, I can be there in 15 minutes :)" I hop in the shower, and I'm quickly scrubbing my arm pits and crotch, just in case anything happens. I'm drying off, and have just a spritz of my cologne, but I plan on burning incense on the way so that I am brimming with fragrances. Like an original Olympian, being bathed in various perfumes, hair and body glistening with olive oil—all to compete for only the virtue, and a simple olive wreath.

We're texting about the location, and I'm already outside Best Buy while she is searching for parking, my face growing rosier with the wind chill. I'm walking towards her, acting as if I don't notice her, and I'm texting her "Oh my god I have to go, a beautiful red head is walking my way :)" Her freshly-dyed hair is so deeply rich, like the sands of Mars or the ripest strawberry. We meet outside Best Buy, and I'm putting my arm around her. I'm telling her how I've missed her, and she's wincing in pain as I unintentionally apply too much pressure to her ribs, my short term memory failing me temporarily. I start to apologize, my eyes widening and almost misting, like a summer's humidity on the verge of breaking. I tell her that I'm sorry, and place both hands on her face and start kissing her, our tongues enveloping the other's for a brief moment, but she's not as into public affection, and wants to go inside. "So what prompted the new phone? Are you having problems getting texts from people?" And I'm asking for myself indirectly.

"Yeah, that and my sister got a new one, and I don't know, it was that time." As we're walking toward the phone section, her gait is wounded, and she's huddling into herself as if she's very cold—but she's not, it's to protect herself.

The salesman that asks us the obligatory "Do you need help finding anything?" stock questions is named Ash. I ask him, "So how are Brock and Misty?"

"What?" He says, and Taylor looks embarrassed.

"Oh, uh, you know, from the cartoon *Pokémon*." I'm laughing and he's resisting smiling, "I couldn't help myself."

"Oh yeah, I hear that all the time," he says, even though it's a lie. He's looking at me with an intensity that is in part jealousy, disgust, and attraction. He's wishing I wasn't here with Taylor,

and that I was into him instead. Every question
she's asking, he's answering and trying to not show
that he's glancing at me. His biology betrays him.
Males have awful peripheral vision, and he drinks
me in these subtle glances—and I like it, and how
jealous he is of me. I wore an especially tight
hoodie both to show off my arms, which are a very
defined 17 inches, and because Taylor likes them
(both my arms and hoodies). On the way, I
pictured her getting chilly in the store, and offering
my hoodie to her like a gentleman—but she never
asks, or actually seems cold. They're talking about
data, switching plans, or transferring plans, trying
to keep a plan. For someone as capricious and
unreliable as Taylor, who has cancelled at the last-
minute numerous times, I find it silly that she's
talking so much about plans. But I love her all the
same. For those three hundred and thirty five days
of the year that she's emotionally withdrawn,
distant, busy, sick, on her period, mildly disgusted,
or overly nostalgic for some memory, and not

lifting a finger to get in touch with me—and not even for the other thirty days where I might see her—I love her.

He says something to her, and she looks over to me seeking an approval of some sort. Maybe I'm supposed to offer to buy it, or I'm supposed to weigh in on something. "Well so what do you think honey, do you want to get it? I can help out, or did you want to go to another store?"

"Yeah, let's keep looking around, but first let's get some lunch."

"Okay, what were you thinking? I could do sushi, or Chinese, or burritos."

"I know of this great Chinese buffet right up the street. We can walk there!" And just like that we're walking up the sidewalk, her staying close to me for warmth whenever there's a cold gust of wind. I say we should get a selfie—she expertly takes the photo, and I look so goofy. I'm telling her to be sure to send it to me. We pick out a table, and I load up my plate.

I know it's a big deal to her that I like this place, and I'm hungry so I keep saying "Oh yeah!" whenever I take a bite of something.

"See, I told you it was good," she says with this wonderfully playful half-smile.

"I'm not a big fan of the green tea, it's just a touch too sweet."

She drinks from my cup, with a familiarity as if we've always known each other. "Tastes okay to me. Oh, and by the way, Budweiser isn't the king of all beers." She's making a comment about my hat, and again, like a freight train, that smile just runs right through me.

"Oh ha, see I just thought this was funny. I don't drink, and I just sort of like wearing it to be—" I cringe at the thought that I almost said to be ironic, "goofy." It's as if I've betrayed something, that a potential bond over drinking vanishes. "So how are you holding up?"

"I'm okay, just a couple weeks of being tender." I'm sitting here mystified by her. I'm picturing always being there for her, in that moment when she rested on my lap. I'm picturing telling her that I love her, that I loved her from the second I laid eyes on her, but I just didn't want to tell her too early and scare her away. And it's dawning on me that this is the first in-person conversation we've had that wasn't prefaced with anything sexual. It worries me, but I'm putting it in the back of my head, focusing on eating and making silly jokes. Toward the end of the meal, she looks down at her phone and furrows her brow.

"Sorry, I just got this text from my mom. I told her not to start her car this morning because the battery is almost dead, and I thought she would get stuck. And that's exactly what happened. It makes me so mad that she did this. She wants me to go jump her car, but I'm not going to." She's looking down and away from me at her phone, glancing off to the side and outside the restaurant.

"Oh no, it's okay, go give her a jump."

"No, I'm pissed that she didn't listen to me. But, I mean, I really should go to her, I think. Are you sure it's okay?"

"Hey, I understand, life happens. Do you want me to go with you? Or do you want to meet up after and go to the mall to look at more phones?"

"Maybe." Our check arrives, and I'm paying for it. She's offering and I'm refusing politely. "Well, thank you for lunch."

"When will I see you again? When is, the hotel happening?" I ask with a big grin.

"How about, Sunday?"

"That works for me." We're both smiling, and I know that it will be soon that I tell her how I feel, that I've been in love with her for some time now. That I'm seeing a future with her. The hotel is when I'll tell her beautiful things—that she is this missing part of me I never knew was missing...

Walking outside, the air is brisk and our hearts are beating rapidly, yet somehow the nervous system in our bodies continue to move our muscles down the pavement. The fires in our souls are whispering to each other, fanning each other. We're outside her car, and I'm squeezing her ass and kissing her, her upper lip being gently sucked into my mouth at the end of each kiss. "I know you have to go, I just want to kiss you a little bit more." Each kiss is an intense rush of blood to my head, the oxytocin overwhelming the synapses of my brain.

"You're greedy," she says, eyes shut, smiling.

"I know," and I take a few more, gingerly holding her before she has to go. I stagger back to my car, keeping her in my sight as I'm walking, always wanting her to be safe and to be able to have my love to carry her. I think of her poor cracked ribs, and her joints that pop from playing sports, and I think of that throwback picture on her Facebook where she's wearing a cast on her leg and her hair has bangs, and I ache for her. I send her a text, "I'm high as a kite right now from your kisses <3 I see now how affected you are from your accident, and I wanted to say for Sunday to not worry about not being able to have sexy times." I've tipped the direction to include more cutesy sweet nothings in addition to the sexual undertones in texts. "I am perfectly content lying in bed with you, kissing you endlessly. I did get worked up though kissing you, lol. I would think you can handle me licking your peach. I'll try not to make you contract your muscles too hard when you orgasm, but I can't guarantee it :)"

I sit there in my car, looking at my phone, waiting for her response. I'm skulking about on her Facebook and within 10 minutes of our date, she puts up a status that says "New phone!" A guy named Luke comments "You're welcome ;)" underneath it. I comment, "Glad you were able to jump your mom's car so fast." My comment is deleted, I'm blocked, and I begin texting her— things are spiraling dangerously out of control. "What the hell is going on? Taylor, I am very upset right now. Look if you don't want another guy to see you talking with me, that's fine. But don't leave me in the dark about it... You know how much I fucking care for you. I never want to hurt you. You need to call me, like, right now... Taylor, I am like fucking in love with you, and you are making a mistake that I don't understand..." It wasn't supposed to be this way... it was supposed to be deep and poetic... "I was texted last night by a girl begging, *begging* me to fuck her. I told her no, and I told her no three separate times, because of how I feel about you... I am hurting right now because my feelings for you are more than friendly, more than sexual, but closer to love. I know that you feel it for me too, don't try to say it isn't so. I know you're seeing someone else, Luke is my guess. I haven't said anything to him, I wasn't planning on it. Why? Because in my pettiness it would only serve to hurt you. And I know how fragile your heart really is, even though you try to hide it. Please just call me." I call her, and hear the sound of an answer and hang up. I start driving recklessly to her house, barely paying attention to the road and my vision is blurry from tears.

"I don't want the other girls... They don't care about me, they just want sex and I hate it :(" I'm really saying that I hate myself, and I keep letting go of any semblance of having it together... "Just talk to me, just have some empathy! ... Don't you dare try to kid yourself into thinking you're a bad person, that you deserve misery, to not be with someone good, don't you fucking dare. I well up with tears when I think about you with him, with anyone else. I have feelings, and emotions, I'm a fucking person. And it's like, you squash my heart in an instant, and then you just make my day in another..." It goes on and on, and I'm at her door, pounding on it. No cars are in her driveway, but I'm beating on the door calling her name, the beautiful name being strangled in my throat... Oh my darling, oh my darling... I've been knocking so hard that my fist hurts, the skin on the backside is cracking. These same hands were inside her just weeks ago. She was telling me how I know exactly where to go, and now my hands are uselessly being bruised on her door.

I go back to sitting in my car, contemplating my next move. I turn my car on getting ready to go back home, defeated. As I'm sitting there, I'm entering into Google "how to know when you're blocked on iPhone". It describes the phone ringing once, going to voicemail, and that any messages you leave won't be recorded. I call her again, and it rings once and goes to voicemail. I tell her that I love her, into the static of the world, realizing she'll never hear it, but that doesn't matter. I just need it to be said out loud for myself—to know that I utter these words into the world. I get home, and I'm writing her sister an e-mail, telling her that I can't be there to watch over her... I'm going past the barrier of desperation, beyond coming back from. As I finish up my e-mail, I feel this foaming, gurgling sensation beneath my windpipe. It's as if something caustic, all my petty jealousy and turpid sadness is mixing in my stomach. Before I realize what's happening, I start throwing up walking toward my bathroom, my hand cupped over my mouth, undigested food and brownish yellow fluid seeping out the sides of my hand. I'm retching, tears streaming down my face and my eyes are completely bloodshot with bursting vessels from the crying and the forcefulness of my vomiting. It's as if some figurative demon has reached into my spine and ripped out my central nervous system, and I've lost all control of my body. Like my uncle Frank, who when he heard his son had died, writhed and cried in such a guttural way that he ended up freezing, and awakening the Parkinson's inside him.

New Year's Eve

It's New Year's Eve, and cliché thoughts run through my head about changing, becoming better for Taylor's sake. Herein lies my core problem—that I don't think of becoming better for myself. I've been dreaming of Taylor, because my mind throbs her name over and over again, and it's like I'm with her again... even though I'm not. The dreams fade when the urge to throw up becomes too overpowering and it wakes me up, it has become overpowering on a daily basis. I'm looking into my toilet, knowing that bile will be coming up soon. Sure enough, I'm throwing up a dark brown fluid, no food, just bile and stomach acids, and when I hear my phone make the incoming text noise, I instinctively bring it up to eye level. I'm not quite adjusted to this newer phone's size, and the case is slicker than I'm used to, and I drop it accidentally into the toilet. I let out a blood-curdling scream, the kind of tragic sound a mother would make at seeing her child die. I reach in, unthinking, to my disgusting toilet, wipe off my phone and quickly put it into a container of rice. Has it always been this way... this piece of silicon and buttons, a little computer meaning so much to me for no reason? While I'm sorting out my pathetic attachment to a cellphone, grateful it still works after the rice treatment dried it out, I'm looking at myself in the mirror before going to work. I again see this inescapable darkness on the horizon. But how dark does it really get? How deep can I sink in the desperation before it brims before the nostrils, filling my lungs... You fall for long enough, get so deep into it, that it doesn't even feel like falling anymore.

Losing My Grip

It's the day after New Year's Day, and I'm texting Taylor with a sense of optimism, telling her how it's a new year and a fresh start for everyone. The cheesy part in me thinks that this will somehow work, that she'll magically forget my desperation. As I always do, I'm rambling to every stranger about her and our situation. They all say the same thing—to ignore her and move on—not realizing the impossibility of such an act for me. My muscle tone feels like jelly, for the last week they've contracted so hard from stress that I've fully exhausted my body. This fact, and my damaged emotional state, aren't stopping me from going to the gym. I'm in an ocean of testosterone. Everyone seems to have made it a point to work their chest today—I'm invigorated by this and decide to hit 300 on the bench. I'm doing 135 for a warmup, my joints sounding like a cement mixer because of a shoulder injury I ignored that healed over terribly. It feels like my coracobrachialis is tight, but I'm doing 225 for reps anyway. I load the bar up to 300 pounds, and have a spotter now, who I'm instructing to allow me to struggle or fail if needed. A calm overcomes me, the bar is lifted off and it feels light. "Do it for yourself," I'm telling myself in my mind. I'm lowering the bar using my lats and thickness of my traps, storing up kinetic energy in my chest on the descent. My hamstrings, glutes, and quadriceps are all contracting in unison with my triceps and pectoral muscles. All that glory is being slowly raised up, and it's more than just overcoming the forces of gravity, it's overcoming life. "Hey that was a good lift, brother," my spotter is saying. "Yeah I got 335 for a triple yesterday, still looking to get 350 this month." Always a dick measuring contest. "You got me beat on the deadlift though, what did you pull the other day?"

"That's right!" I say, "620." The endorphins and adrenaline are subsiding, being replaced by cortisol... All these hormones... oxytocin bonded me and Taylor, and I feel my body catabolizing...

I'm stripping the weights, and there's a natural alpha male, who's also on a steroid stack, next to me. His stance is wide, blocking the weight tree. As I look at him, I wonder if my underdeveloped glutes make me appear like a lazy fuck, or if my lack of a lat spread shows that I'm not a provider, and if this is the subconscious reason that girls lose interest in me. I would give anything to have been born a big dicked jock. I think about him, someone who could fuck Taylor, and he wouldn't mind never hearing from her again. How she would give him head, surrender herself to him, and he wouldn't even give a shit. He'd just be moving from moment to moment, person to person, and I'm no better on my worst days. And I'm thinking of her with any man who isn't me, I'm holding on to a 45 pound plate, with one hand, and I'm unconsciously dropping it on my big toe from hip height. "Oh," I say, not even feeling it happen. I'm in the locker room, on the verge of tears when a guy walks in.

"What's up" he says, looking at my bloody

sock.

"Ah I dropped a weight on my toe like a fucking idiot."

"Oooh, damn, that must have hurt."

I'm picturing Taylor's lips on mine, her on my lap when I say, "yeah it did". I'm calling work to say to my boss, "Hey man, I cut my toe, and I am running behind. I got to get something to make it stop bleeding. Should only be like, 10 minutes late." I'm asking the pharmacist at CVS what I should do, if just gauze and an ace bandage would do the trick.

"You need to go to the hospital, right away" she says, terrified.

"Really, you think so? Oh man, I'm sorry, I didn't realize I was bleeding on your floor." A pool is forming beneath my shoe. "I didn't feel anything when I dropped the weight on it."

"No, you need to go, that's not going to

stop bleeding." I'm calling my boss, and telling him I won't be able to come in tonight, and I'm asking him how to get to an Urgent Care center. I'm so lost.

If It Ain't Broke, Don't Fix It

I'm in the hospital waiting room, casually looking at porn on my phone on silent. It's just softcore massaging, a woman being covered in oil and fingered slowly—anything to not think about Taylor anymore. The wait isn't too long, and my foot is being gingerly taken care of by someone I went to high school with. He doesn't seem to recognize me. "So like, I probably could've just not come in right?"

"Well, do you like having two feet?"

"Well yeah, but I mean, even if I broke it, there's nothing you can really do anyway for a broken toe, is there?"

"I can tell you that you did break your toe."

"Oh no."

"This type of fracture is actually extremely prone to infection. And this is what would've happened if you would've waited to come in.

About a week from now, you would've noticed discoloration and pain and would have to come in because of the pain. Then, we would cut off your big toe. Except, bad news, we didn't get it all by cutting off just your toe. So, now we cut off this part of your foot—" he motions a slice at the base of all my toes—" and maybe we get it all. Or maybe we need to cut it right here—" and this time he slices my foot in half—"and you basically—"

"—have a stump at that point."

"Pretty much."

"Well I'm definitely glad I didn't try to man through this, or whatever." Another doctor comes in, older, tired looking, with glasses at the end of his nose, as if he's too drained to push them back up, or to get a new prescription. He's washing my toe to prepare it for injections of contact anesthetic, he's pushing in deep with a needle and I still don't feel anything. He's sewing my toenail back into the nailbed, to prevent infection. I'm looking at him—focusing, recalling the muscle memory of stitching up countless people. I see behind his eyes a life lived, studied and evenly tempered, a ring on his finger showing through the glove. He'll mention to his wife about his day being long, and he'll listen to her talk about her day... and it all seems so impossible to me. I'm leaving, picking up my antibiotics, not thinking about the medical bill that will be on the way, or being out of work for a few months, because my mind is only a bellowing blare of Taylor. I'm wearing the same hoodie I had on when we last saw each other, cursing myself for having gum in my pocket. The spearmint is covering up any trace of her scent from our embrace. I'm twirling around a hair in its pocket, I have been every time I wear it since I saw her last. This is all I have left of her. I started chewing the gum each day, wanting to be close to the moment when I saw her last, and now I'm mourning the last piece of gum in my pocket. I chew it a little bit, take it out while it's still malleable and sticky, and wrap Taylor's hair inside it, really cover it up. I'm chewing on it a little, and I swallow... just wanting her to be a part of me one more time...

I'm on crutches the next few weeks, and each day I'm not working I enthusiastically tell myself, "I'm going to get so much done today." Yet all my spare time is spent messaging random girls on OkCupid. I'm playing up the fact that I broke my toe, and hoping to get a pity lay. I'm telling them how I'm taking advantage of it, cleaning up my place, reading books, using the time to my advantage. They don't need to know that time is a punishment, and memories the tormentor. They don't need to see the cobwebs expanding beyond a cute unlit corner, the dishes with rotting food in the sink, the toilet bowl stained with bile and vomit, pubic hair scattered on the floor from when I shaved for Taylor, the piss stains on the floor from when I stopped caring about dignity... I can't move on from any of this...

Getting Back In the Pink

I'm talking with a big titted blonde girl who likes anal sex, and I'm wondering how much work I need to put in before that can happen. We're both raving about sushi, and I'm pacing around my room while texting her. I'm just starting to feel comfortable with walking in boots, steel toed after too many people stepped on my foot. We both overshare before our date. She's telling me about how the last guy she liked drugged and raped her, gave her a pregnancy scare, and that it took her a long time to get over him. I'm telling her that I care too much, that it pains me that happened to her, and that I want to help the only way I know how by making her feel good and cared for. When she replies the next day that it was only because she was "drunk lol" to downplay what she confessed, and glosses over it, I'm relieved. We're on a date and it's going amazingly, despite the fact the sushi restaurant is using candied fryer fat, from the oil needing changed. Her palate can't detect this, and

124

it bothers me that she likes it so much. She's talking, and I'm laughing and smiling, telling her stories, making fun of our waiter and her eyes are dilating, her cheeks are getting flushed, and I sense her pussy starting to drip into her panties. She's wanting me to grope her here in the restaurant, squeeze those triple D's right here in front of everyone while she moans. Only I believed her when she said she wanted to take things slow. I'm here with the intent of just having a nice meal and enjoying her cleavage and dimples, and when her chubby cheeks and lips form a smile, I picture her dutifully sucking cum out of my throbbing cock. I'm outside with her, she's talking about her Mustang and how much she loves it. Yes, you move fast, and it's all you and I know and crave. She starts her car, and she's telling me that I should definitely text her, and that we need to have another date. My phone dies, and I drive home with the rush of feeling wanted, and I'm touching myself at red lights thinking about torturing her with the endless giving of pleasure and how deeply I would tongue her ass. The next day I'm texting her that I had so much fun talking, that I wasn't ignoring the many texts she sent me that night, but that my phone died. Then she tells me that she's not ready to be dating now, even though she's still on OkCupid. She's still looking for that person to break her again, force himself on her, because that's all she's good for in her mind. I'm telling her, uselessly, that I see more in her than she does. That she deserves good things. She blocks me on the site, and I'm glad I don't have to see her face anymore. We are too similar—emotional masochists looking for spiritual sadists.

The prowling continues, and grows more desperate with each passing day. I'm finding myself barely able to function, and all of my free time is devoted to online dating, to prevent the realization of my failures with Taylor from coming to a head. I smile and say "I'm doing great, how about yourself?" to people when they ask me how it's going, even though inside me entire cities of memories are being demolished and raging fires are engulfing my soul. Sometimes I'm running out of breath waiting for a free moment to do more match searches. I narrow the field down to 18 to 22 year olds within 100 miles in the hopes that Taylor has a new profile and that I can message her again... that maybe somehow she wants me to contact her again. Her phone number changed and she deleted her Facebook, I tell myself. I start thinking too much about the way she tastes, about the way her eyes look like they have a world inside them, and how I should've grabbed her bowl that first night and smoked with her to show her I could be adventurous and fun. I start chatting it up with Christina, a girl who's interested in psychology, and she works in a prison talking to the inmates, and it's the same story with just different details. A girl that wound up getting fucked too young, and is seeking a way to find that man again. But she disguises this by saying the human mind fascinates her, and that she's lived through a lot, and that she thinks she can really help people. But it's her open sexuality that I care about. She's overweight (or as she lists on her profile, "curvy"), and bigger girls always give the best head because they feel the need to make up for their own perceived lack of attractiveness. If she's anything like myself, she's also desperate to please and get someone else off. I spend the afternoon cleaning my place as best as I can. She comes over, cleavage spilling out of her top, and I start massaging her, working up from her feet that smell of talcum (as in she skipped a shower after work), up to her shoulders. Now I'm feeling her up on my couch, disinterestedly, while *Hell's Kitchen* plays on my TV softly. I start fondling her breasts, pushing them up and cupping them into a more appealing shape than they naturally have. I pass on sucking on them, deciding that it's too intimate, and I don't want her to feel a bond with me. Her pussy is actually quite nice, maintained, and tight. She doesn't seem to get

128

very wet like I usually get girls, but it may be because of the awkward angle of lying on my couch. I think for a second about telling her that I want her on my bed, but I'm just going through the motions of fingering her, listening to the sounds of my couch springs being overworked, and something overcomes me. I want to give her everything, as fast and as hard and rough as I can, until pure exhaustion settles in, and then I want her to suck my cock. I give her my all, she cums, my arm and wrist and fingers are aching with abuse. I tell her that I want head.

"Nah, you're all sweaty now. Nobody wants to suck a sweaty dick." And she laughs after saying this.

"Aw man, dang, I should've asked for the blowjob first!" Her head is getting clear, she's looking around at my place as she goes to use the toilet. I pace by hoping to hear her still in my bathroom, and I grab a towel from my bedroom to get some of the sweat off, hopeful she'll notice a difference and get down on all fours.

"So I need to get going, early morning and all."

"Oh, so soon? Okay, well let me tell you how to get back on to 83 from here, because it can be tricky."

"I have my GPS." She says, curtly, and just like that she tells me I have nothing that interests her, that this was a mistake. That all I had to offer her was on my couch.

Oh My Darling

"Still sits on my desk, and every day I see that beautiful face." I look at my phone three times, still unsure if I'm perhaps in a dream, but sure enough, it's her. My Darling, Taylor, sending me a picture of Max, my pug. We talked about her dog Max, and mine with his poor crooked jaw and his long tongue hanging out, and about us being in bed all together, just being together like a happy family. She was the only one I felt close enough with to tell that dream to. I included his picture in her Christmas bundle, and so many feelings come rushing towards me from her text that I don't even know what to say. So I send her another picture of Max, and tell her how much he would love to meet her. I hope silently, that she knows this isn't a guilt trip, but rather a statement of the purity of dogs and their ability to love unconditionally.

"Well so how have you been? I haven't stopped thinking about you, and hoping you're doing okay." Too available, but too late.

"Actually I've been sick :/"

"Oh you poor thing!" I desperately write back, and text in short flurries of sentences. "I oughta make you soup, I make a mean chicken corn noodle haha."

"Oh God, that sounds good right now, but I'm at work lol."

"Ah I see." I think back to when I had delivered flowers to her house, how I thought about sending them to her work instead, but didn't want her to think it was weird. When I brought that up, she said she would've loved that. And I'm already in the store picking up chopped red onions, celery, sweet corn, a roasted chicken, whole carrots, shredded cheddar cheese, salted butter, several containers of chicken stock, and hearty egg noodles. I love the idea of showing up to her work tomorrow, soup in hand, and surprising her. I have the foresight to see that this is a bad idea—too aggressive with caring in the past has pushed her

132

away—but I can't even see, too blinded by the intense love for her bursting behind my eyes. I'm telling her that I hope she feels better, and that I'll talk to her tomorrow, and I'm standing at my kitchen sink by the Crock Pot, happily chopping up carrots, sliding off and cutting off pieces of chicken, and sitting down to collect my thoughts as the scents and spices fill my trailer.

The entire drive I'm feeling her, the anticipation of surprising her, realizing that I don't know if she even likes surprises. I'm shaking as I pull into the parking lot of her work, and I casually text her a picture of the soup, letting her know that I'm there with it. No response. I think back to a picture I saw of her on Facebook, which I viewed from my fake account because she blocked me, in which she's wearing headphones while filing away medical records. Ah, she probably didn't hear her phone go off... I'm texting her again, telling her that I'm coming up to give her soup. My chest is tightening, my muscles tensing, and I feel the release of adrenaline in my body. An evolution of tangible superhuman strength to avoid predators, or to kill them, reduced to the start of a flood of hormones when in love or stressed at work. I see her name on the call registry for employees, and I get a thrill at calling her up.

"Hello?"

"Yes, is this Taylor?"

"Yes it is." There's a slight moment where even she is unsure why she's being asked, as if this phone had never rung for her outside of co-workers.

"This is uh, this is Sean. I've got soup for you, I made it homemade for you and have some gifts too."

"No, oh my God you didn't." She makes her way to me. She seems giddy, and I'm relieved. She appears from behind a double door, and just like the first time I saw her, I'm completely decimated. My central nervous system is over-firing, my muscles tightening, my face is blushing, and I'm trembling but I'm able to hide it. It's a terrible wonderful thing being in love. She's hugging me, and I'm kissing her. Kissing and being intimate somehow always supersedes my usual phobia of germs. "So look, if you're able to hang around for a little bit, I can take my lunch with you." She's smiling, and it's radiant. "Can you stick around for a half-hour?"

"Absolutely... I can go get something to drink for myself."

"If you really want to be an enabler, you could always get me a pack of smokes."

"Of course, anything else? Maybe a drink?"

"No, I have my water," and she laughs, and I revel in seeing her smile again. I drive around, absorbing her town, breathing it in. I'm at some sort of farmer's market, seeing various breads and cheeses, and I wish my stomach could still handle all these delights. It dawns on me that I don't remember her favorite cigarettes—Marlboros in a green box, but not the regular menthols, a mental note I made.

"Honey, what kind of smokes do you want? I know it's a special menthol..."

"Marlboro Smooths. And I prefer hundreds! <3" I pull my I.D. out, the problem of having a cute and young looking face (although it's fading in its cuteness as I age) is always being carded. I'm driving back to her, pounding my fist into the ceiling of my car in excitement.

"Thank you so much," she says, hugging me, and I'm kissing her again. I would always bitch at my parents for smoking in the car, telling them to roll the window down more. "Not when the AC is on" they would say. And yet I'm intoxicated by her mentholated mouth, the smoke filling the air and soothing me with its familiarity. With just one huff of those hundreds of carcinogens and nicotine and rotten poison, I'm taken away to summer days at the family camp in Raystown, my stepdad smoking while fishing; I'm taken back to Cat smoking after orgasm; back to my Grandma in Georgia smoking, telling me how much I look like my dad, and how she wished I could've seen him. It's paradise in just a few seconds.

"So what the heck happened?" I say, still wanting to know, needlessly.

"I'm really sorry. I've been messed up for a while. My one boyfriend really messed me up, and I'm still trying to get past it. I started talking to someone, a therapist, about it."

"Well, I have to give you credit, you're doing more than I am. I could probably stand to talk to someone too. I just mean, I know there's something here between us. I haven't been with anyone since you. Well I went on a date, and I fingered a girl at my place."

"That's it?"

"You're the one I really want."

"Well, I do think you're amazing. You're very nice, and sweet, and if I could be with anyone, it'd be you. I'm just not in the right place right now, and it might take a while until I am."

"That's all I really needed to hear."

Her phone goes off, and she smiles a little. "This is my girl toy, she's jealous I'm having lunch with you. She's lucky that she's fucking gorgeous," and she laughs.

"So you started seeing someone?" I feel like my mom, just dying to know all the details about her life.

"Well friends are what's really important for me right now, and she's just someone I can mess around with from time to time." Something safer than the man who scared her, non-committal and easy. Most likely what she feels about me, and she wouldn't be wrong—at least about the easy part. I only require a little grain of attention, and give eternities of affection in return.

138

"Well you know I care for you."

"I do."

"And you know I told you that my hands were my gift to you, but really, it's my heart. It's like a planet." We start walking toward her car to drop off my gifts and her soup, because she's saving it for later. We're sitting on the curb, she's lighting another cigarette up. There's some force between us, that magnetism of life that brought me to a person that I can be calm and silent with. Normally, I talk a lot without saying what I mean to say. I tell her this, that sometimes it's just easier for me to communicate physically. And it dawns on me, that most of what was truly said between us was said on her bed—my hands making her ache, and her taking it all. I was her beast, and she is the beauty that could tame me. We never really had a lot of common interests, but I felt like I could be a good person when I was around her. That's the best part of being in love—it doesn't need explanation or evidence or common ground to be real. And for the briefest of moments, we weren't two separately ruined people, instead we joined in a union, and our twin flames burned as one. She is beautiful, and not in the simple biological accident way—like a pearl, which is nothing more than an irritation being covered. There was something broken and sad inside her and it shows in the way she smokes her Marlboros, that she takes her time with them as they're a reprieve from her demons. She is unpretentious, a tomboy, and like myself trying to sift through pleasures trying to find traces of love. My heartbeat would be forever irregular because of meeting her, and it would be hard to breathe at the deafening thought of her name. Our attraction was based on nothing tangible, as if it was so big that it was born out of the stars themselves.

"When can I see you again?"

"I'm not sure, but soon," she says, as office workers are walking by us. I start kissing her, caressing her tongue with mine and grabbing her ass. I love you for all the things I'm not and never will be, and I love you for not thinking I'm some weird pervert, and I am the moon to your sun and I'm grateful to have ever met you. Some people are the air in your lungs, don't you know... that's what you've been to me... I think these things, and instead I tell her that I'll see her later. There are so many things to be said for time, and how it interferes with fully living our lives. It's a vast space that I look out on, going on and on forever, and in the moment, I don't consider that I won't have new opportunities to talk with her, even though I know it's all always ending. The genius who has a Eureka moment, and fails to write it down. I must believe that I'll see her tomorrow, or next month, or next year, and that our lives will intersect and orbit with each other once more. I'm feeling a pain in my big toe, where I broke it while thinking of her with another, the phantom pain of a true love always being with me on humid days. I'm texting her later that day, telling her that I am invigorated and rejuvenated by her kisses, and she never responds. I know it's over... and yet I want to believe for just a little longer that I'll hear back from her. Oh my Darling, mein liebling... ich liebe dich, ich liebe dich.

Master and Slave

There's a spark in the vacuum of space, and with it, entire galaxies are born into emptiness. This spark of life resides in the atoms of the smallest microorganisms of a germ, melding itself to specks of dirt, surviving miraculously, and is new. Existence itself evolving out of the bacterial oceanic salinity to land, untold countless destinies being fulfilled. Life begins breathing through the very life essence that existed in the beginning of the universe, unknowingly a part of one entity of elements that exists in the present and the millennia of the past. A great, fated homogeny of breath and evolving, immeasurable and sufferable lifetimes rising to pinnacles only to be outpaced by other species, until man is formed. Lightning crashes, striking a branch to catch fire, and man sees this, understands this, replicates this. Enlightenment happens, Renaissances, Crusades, sonnets are written, Galileo looks through his telescope, Michelangelo chisels visible veins into David, empires collapse, there are feasts and famines, Mozart exists, medicine is studied and botched and butchered until ingenious cures are discovered, beasts are tamed and traded, oceans are explored by understanding the stars and the relationship to direction, Tesla is inventing alternating current, Baron Von Steubon is training sturdy American men in the early winters, Marie Curie wins two Nobel Prizes in different sciences, Edison is furiously creating, people are putting flowers on Chopin's tombstone to this day, the spark of a combustion engine as a key turns and the freedom it implies... All that wondrous and destined time on earth, the generations of lives that outlived disease and famine, languages being developed and lost, artists going mad, that spark... that fire... all of it being disregarded as my thumb scrolls through pictures of girls on Tinder, just trying to find someone easy to fuck. Not for

144

procreation, not even for pleasure at this point, but just succumbing to the inevitable murky waters of casual sex—the methadone for love—anything to not feel heartache any longer. A disgraceful disappointment to the eons of evolution and ancestry.

I burn through 2.5 gigabytes of data within a week of swiping right nonstop. I can always filter out the ones I'm not interested in later. A memory floats back to me, our first family computer only had 1 gigabyte of memory, and how laughable it was that it would ever be filled up. I match with an older woman, who doesn't beat around the bush, but makes it obvious that's all she really wants. She gives me her number easily, and I realize she's only doing what I do, throwing out a big net, but for different reasons. I'm doing it so I don't get hurt over just one person, and she's doing it because it doesn't matter who's fucking her, so long as someone is.

"How big is your dick?"

"Average"

"The fuck is average?"

"Six inches"

"Oh okay, that isn't too small."

Bored, and disinterestedly, I ask "do you like anal?"

"It's okay. Just ease it in my ass."

"And you'll swallow?"

"Yeah, but sometimes I want you to cum inside my pussy. I really want to do a threesome, with you and another girl." Wanting to transition to experimenting in a safer, non-threatening way.

"Maybe someday, I don't even know your full name, haha."

"What do you mean someday? I want it this week. Look I'm trying to get all these things done before I get into a serious relationship. I don't have time for this faggot shit." I let a few minutes pass, stunned in a way before her final

146

exchange. "Ha, as if I'd let you fuck me with that little dick."

I keep swiping, going through an endless litany of girls looking for Instagram followers, girls saying they're not looking for a hookup (how they write that seriously is astonishing), girls wanting beards and other vague descriptions of their father figures, teenage girls with kids saying they aren't easy and to swipe left if I think they are. One girl is going on telling me that my tattoo doesn't really mean "sweetheart"—she's supposedly from Russia. I'm checking on Google translate to be sure, and see it can also mean expensive—she has money on her mind. Another girl wants me to make a cum tribute video for her, and jerk off and film it while calling her a worthless slut and treating her like a sex object, which I do as she's sending me sexy pictures. "Nice cumshot," she says. I also send her an older video I shot a few years earlier when I was doing Kegels more regularly, and she says "mmm" and I never hear from her again. There are girls

147

advertising trips to Europe that I could never fathom having enough money for in my lifetime. None of them are what I really want, but I'm saying yes anyway. I further take the edge off with my daily dose of Wellbutrin. I come across, like a desert oasis for the thirsty, a beautiful ivory brunette. There's something unique about her pictures, which I'm studying for several minutes before messaging her. Unlike other girls her age, who are more interested in staging pictures that document their lives rather than living it, hers seem to tell a story of someone living in the moment. One picture shows her standing in Hawaiian waters. Her cheeks slightly blushing, almost cherub like, and somehow the photographer captured a genuine moment of happiness between her and a friend. She wasn't posing merely to give others the impression that her life is amazing. Genuine smiles activate different muscles of the face than fake smiles, which is why fake ones are always so garish. Nothing seems forced in her features, and even in a top that shows cleavage, she owns it triumphantly and doesn't have a trace of desperation. Her selection of pictures is carefree, unlike my specific and planned selection of pictures: A picture of me smirking with a plate of sushi to show I'm an adventurous eater (and to say, "what can I say? I love to eat :P" when girls comment on the size of the plate); a picture of me and Max, my pug, so that girls have something adorable to fawn over and associate it subconsciously with me; and an artistic muscular pose to subtly show off my body, while also proudly marking my achievements in weight loss. We miraculously match, even though she seems much too attractive to be swiping right at random... She could have anyone she wants. She seems so effortlessly easy going, and for the first time in a while, I approach someone with actual effort instead of just hurling sex at them.

"Hey, it's nice to meet you, Sabrina, my name is Sean :D I think you're incredibly adorable, and my God those eyebrows are perfect. And I simply must know about your trip to Hawaii! Also, do you like sushi?? Clearly I do, haha. I look forward to hearing more about you :)" And I leave for the gym, hopeful about her. I'm going through radio stations, when "Get Lucky" by Daft Punk comes on the radio, and it's a weaker station that's getting lost in the static... but I just want to be close to the idea of Taylor again, remembering that she loved this song. The radio fuzz shifts and replaces "Get Lucky" with another song that recycles some vaguely familiar beat and timing structure, as if to say this is close enough to what you want to hear, and like with relationships, you should move on, as none of this is meant to last. But I wonder still about "Get Lucky"—why did she like it? Was she a Daft Punk fan like myself? Was it playing in a club, that night she texted me a picture of her in a dress, and did its rhythm touch her? Was it playing as she left that club, rolling on molly to have unrepeatable casual sex? Would she ever know I wouldn't judge her for it? Was it the obvious double entendre, or did it just make her happy? What music touched her in the places I couldn't? I'm sitting outside the gym, wiping a tear away as I'm making the switch to the gym mentality. I'm not there, merely going through the motions, checking my phone in between reps. The music playing in the weight room is metal, and it's overbearing in its sanitized generic sound, it's playing to replace mental focus with artificial focus... and to drown out conversations to the point that it's only shallow small talks between gym rats, nothing too intimate for fear of knowing someone beyond weight lifting. I set up 300 pounds on the bench press and picture Sabrina. I bet she has those perfectly pink nipples, and I'm sure she's going to squirt with me. I push out three solid reps, and start talking to someone about mobility work and cardio to help bring oxygen to tissues to expedite recovery, but my mind is still on her. I'm aware the obsession is beginning, and I can't do anything about it... I can't remember if I've taken my Wellbutrin, so I take one just in case.

During my set on the bench, she responds to my message. "Oh my god, thank you so much for saying that about my eyebrows! No one's ever said anything about them before, but I do pride myself on them haha. And yes, I love sushi and you're the adorable one :)"

I answer back too quickly, "No one's complimented you on your eyebrows before?! That's a crime! Haha, I think they're underrated in terms of their importance." Soft, easy, and playful—too deep of a conversation will be too much pressure. "Okay, so I have some more questions then!"

"Ask away :)"

"So, are you a fan of massages? What about cuddling? Ahaha, I'm a cuddle monster."

"Yes of course I love massages haha, who wouldn't? And I'm definitely a cuddler!"

"Hey, you'd be surprised, some people don't like massages, they're weirdos haha. I do tend to get a little handsy with cuddling though, I can't help it. :P"

"Oh I'm more than okay with that ;)"

"Really, so you wouldn't mind my hands endlessly caressing you?"

"Not at all."

"So, tell me about Hawaii, it looks incredible."

"It was, I went with my best friend. It's so beautiful there," she says, in a way that I know is so simple because she was awed by it, rather than because she isn't able to come up with a better description. She's describing by feeling.

"I have a confession. I have been waiting to hear back from you because you're so damn cute. I couldn't even focus at the gym."

"Well you could've fooled me with those

arms :)"

"Ahh that's the best thing you could've said haha, you're perfect. Hey here's my number, text me :)" That easily, we're texting, and it evolves quickly into sexting. I'm telling her about kissing the back of her neck, while fondling her breasts, and she's touching herself at the thought. Within a few days, I have pictures of her in cute thongs, pictures of her at work lifting her shirt up to show her bra, and our texting frequency is near constant. I'm at work, sneaking off to the bathroom to take shirtless pictures for her, and texting her while people are talking to me and I'm being an asshole and barely registering them talking to me. "And you'll look up into my eyes while you're sucking my cock, won't you?"

"Of course I will :)"

"And you'll be okay sitting on my face, rubbing your tiny pussy over my lips as you grind and cum on me?"

154

"Mmm, yes please." She goes from being cute to overtly sexual without getting upset about it or feeling bad about herself or making me feel bad about myself. All too often, one party will be very into sexting, usually early on into talking because they're genuinely excited over discovering that part about themselves, only to feel vaguely guilty later—because of the pep talk they give them self when they get one-and-done'd about how they wouldn't do that again, and how they are letting down all those platitudes about not being broken just because they're alone and how they're stronger by themselves. We decide to meet Friday, and that if all goes well, we'll cuddle up in a motel, but we both know it will be more than that. She lives at home, just outside of State College. I wonder if she has that part in her, that always feels like she's looking into the bigger city enviously, half a part of it, wanting to escape fully into it. I don't mind the drive, but I'm borrowing my mom's car because I'm worried about mine breaking down and not getting the chance to get her off, and I'm worried that she'll take someone else up on hanging out instead. She asks me to pull up at the end of her driveway, and she quickly gets in and she's saying "Okay let's get out of here, quickly please."

I drive out of her development, and at a stop sign I put the car in park. I turn to her and see subtle hints of makeup, a tight top, and her breasts are bigger than her pictures would have me believe. She smells nice, mostly like nothing, but traces of her natural body odor and a subtle perfume. Her voice is girlish, but not in an annoying childish way—she has a fun laugh and she's a giggly personality type. I'm kissing her, her tongue is on mine, and we're both flooding with hormones. "You smell nice."

"No I barely had time to get ready," she says and laughs, and it dawns on me that she's stoned. She's not stoned out of her mind, but I picture her nervous about meeting me, about wanting me badly, and wanting to take the edge off.

"So why the hurry at your place?"

"I'm sorry, I just didn't want to explain that I was going out with a guy to my dad."

"Oh, I see, so what do you say?" And I'm smiling, "Still want to go to the hotel?"

"Definitely," she says, and smiles.

"So I'm not some terrible kisser then, I take it?" I say at a red light. I start kissing her again, and this time I'm kissing and licking her neck while I grope her chest.

"Not at all, you're amazing."

"Eh, you could use some work" and I'm laughing obnoxiously, but playfully obnoxious. She's laughing too, knowing that it was just playful teasing without me having to painfully explain. "So what attracted you to me?"

"Everything. You're very handsome, and

funny, and you have good grammar and spelling when texting."

"Isn't that the worst? It's like... You can be an otherwise perfect ten, but if you can't put a sentence together, I completely lose interest."

"And I also like that you think I'm smart too. A couple of guys have underestimated my intelligence."

"Well, some people are just projecting their own lack of intelligence or personality onto you then. Hey! I heard this insane thing the other day." I'm talking, but not making eye contact as I'm focused on driving, wanting to make sure she's safe. "Did you know the word 'gullible' isn't even in the dictionary?"

"Why would—" she giggles, "—wow Sabrina, go from talking about how smart you are to falling for that."

"Ah don't worry about it, you're still adorable." And we both laugh, "But I know you're

158

smart. You just fell for my charming smile and cheesy joke."

"I'm just a little tired," she says with a giggle, not realizing I know she's stoned. We pull into the Stevens Hotel, the reservation already made. I wonder if the clerk knows, that I have a girl I'm going to do debauched things with in the room, that the wetness she'll feel when changing the bedding will be from her pussy gushing from my hands. "Yeah, I'm probably just going to be an hour or so, I'm on a road trip just looking to take a nap," I'm saying to the clerk, and I'm loving the secret between us, she knows, but she doesn't know. "You know how that goes, when you start to get drowsy behind the wheel and it's like, well, better pull over before I hurt someone." We both laugh, and the clerk is telling me a story about a trip she took somewhere, she's smiling at me and putting her hair behind her ear—if not for having eyes for Sabrina, I'd ask for her number. I'm leaving the office, and for the first time I can really take in Sabrina standing outside wearing yoga pants, and she's everything I could ever hope for. Following her, seeing that perfectly shaped eighteen year old ass in too-tight of yoga pants casually walking to our room, thinking back to just a few minutes earlier when she let out a moan as I licked her neck like a wild animal at stop lights on the way. There was no mystery, like the ache when a woman bends down and hints of cleavage are exposed and you catch glances. No, we were both sluts in love and wanting to fuck, and I liked it.

We're kissing, and my hands are on her crotch, caressing her over her pants. I tell her to take off her shirt, in a direct tone, and it turns her on so much that it's palpable. Once she has her shirt off, I can't wait anymore, and I take her right tit out and start sucking on her nipple. Her eyes close, her hand on my head, and I'm looking up at her cheeks getting rosy, her body getting warmer. "Turn off the lights" she says, as a soft question. I do, she takes her top off, and lies back on the bed.

160

Both breasts are beautiful mounds of teenage perfection, and I'm pressing them together, tightly suckling the nipples, switching back and forth, covering them with saliva while my hand is palming her pussy. Her knees are coming together, moving apart, and coming together the closer I get her to orgasm. I spread them apart with a little force, to which she lets out a soft moan.

"You're going to want to stop me, when I start fingering you, because you'll feel something build to a type of orgasm that you've never experienced before, but you don't want to stop me, do you trust me?"

"Okay, yes," she says, nodding. I'm removing her yoga pants, and I pull down her panties to see a bunch of small cuts around her panty line. "They're stretch marks," she says. I tell her, "Shh, it's okay" and kiss her right on her clit. I swirl my tongue on it and lap up inside her pussy, only just to tease her. I move my lips back up to hers as one finger goes in her pussy. I'm kissing

161

her, telling her to taste herself on my lips. She does, she likes it, and she whimpers right as the second finger goes inside her. Two loving and strong fingers start to stroke her G-spot, which isn't tucked too far inside her—every girl is ever so slightly different.

I pull them out, "Now suck on them. Get them nice and wet for fingering your pussy."

"Will you, call it my cunt? I... like cunt," she says softly, shy about the request.

"Taste your cunt on my fingers." She sucks on them, and her drool is covering them. We're both too far gone in the moment and feel animalistic. I start thrusting my fingers up inside her, faster as she starts to squirt on the bed and her legs are starting to close again, but I look at her and she relaxes them, allowing herself to gush everywhere. It's getting on the bed, on me, and on her. Something about her marking me—and the power I have over her with the ease of getting her off overwhelms me, and I walk slightly away from the bed to take my pants off. "Where are we going?" she says, as I shove my cock in her mouth, and she dutifully starts to suck. She's good, not making a blowjob feel like it's a job, and I'm rubbing her tiny, hairless pussy.

"Do you want to cum again?" She nods yes. "I want you to beg me for it."

"Please, baby, please make me cum again. I'm begging you!" She pleads and moans as she's saying it, as I'm already starting to finger her, with my cock still throbbing in front of her face. She squirts again. I move her to her stomach, and spread her ass and start to lick her pussy up to her asshole.

"Do you like that?"

"I do..."

"Tell me you want me to tongue your asshole."

"Tongue my asshole..." she says in ecstasy. My tongue is as deep inside her as possible, fingers pounding away at her G-spot again. She cums again, I think she's cum forty times in the half hour we've been here. We lay down, both in exhaustion, but it's not for long until I have to start licking her clit. I didn't give her enough lip service yet, as I'm licking she's grinding into me. I'm suckling her clit now, keeping a tight seal around it, not bullshitting around lapping at it. She cums over and over, and she's in a state of near shock from the amount of body trembling she's endured. We both are too tired to move, and she puts her arm over my chest, looking up at me with both adoration and admiration. The oxytocin floods our bodies, her pupils are wide and she's falling deeper in love. "When you told me earlier to let it happen, I almost stopped you."

"I know."

"And I'm glad that I didn't. And I was a little stoned earlier, I just didn't know how you felt about it. Some people are very mean."

"I know you were stoned, it's okay." I let out a laugh, "I think it's cute."

"They aren't stretch marks, I used to cut." I see the beginnings of tears form, but she reels them back in.

"It's okay, but I don't want you to do that honey. I'm here now, I'll take care of you."

"And keep me safe?"

"Yes honey." We're starting to fall asleep, both our restless spirits finally calmed, when she remembers that she has to go home. She's standing up. "There's just one more thing I've been dying to try with you. You just stand right there." I drop to my knees, and start licking her pussy and clit again as she stands, and she's trembling so hard she needs to balance herself on me.

"Holy shit, you're just too good at everything," she says, after cumming one last time.

"You don't mind that I want to please a lot, and I'm a little shyer about myself?"

"Not at all, who would be?" She says, almost angry, and I'm angry in a way too, that it's not as appealing to some people as I would have imagined.

"Okay, let's get you home. And hey, what do you have me in your phone as? I have a heart symbol next to your name!" And I laugh, then let out a little burp on accident.

"Adorable," she says, declaratively about my burp. "Here, we'll put you in as this." I watch her fill my contact information with endless multicolored hearts, and I realize that I know how to give her orgasms with ease to the point that merely touching her makes her tremble. I was given that gift, and I already love her. But I don't understand her, and it's wonderful. It's new and mysterious, and I have the pleasure of her showing me who she is in these little windows.

I'm not wanting it to be over. We're driving back, pressed for time by some unknown constraint, and she's nestling into my arm, which is swollen with blood from fingering her so intensely. The oxytocin is flooding our minds, tiring my eyes on the drive, and endearing me to her. We're parked at the base of her driveway, kissing softly, and she's revealing in her lips that she's not one to kiss her partner. It is too intimate, more intimate than the callous nature of the rough one-night stands she's used to. She releases herself to me in the moment, and I to her. Euphoria takes over. The world seems warmer somehow. She's getting out of my car, and walking up her driveway. A swelling of gratitude rises from my chest, my eyes taking in this being who is so pure in her desire for affection that she chose me. And maybe we've both been down all the wrong roads, and made terrible decisions and fucked up at every turn to get here—but here we are perfect.

Budding Bonds

Pure bliss takes over as I'm driving home, and the sense of restlessness fades with each passing mile. I'm looking beyond the road, past the lighting of the truckers' headlights as they're trying to make deliveries on time, past my arrival at home, and I'm facing my life. I'm twenty-seven and going to be thirty soon, an age that always seemed unrealistic... I have been living under the impression that something would have happened by now—some marker of accomplishment. A job I love, a girlfriend, a place that didn't feel so lonely. I feel the loud thuds of my heart calm to a soft melodic humming, and I feel time slowing down. Hope, that feeling of believing in what has never been experienced can still happen, circulates through my body. I'm seeing someone new I can love, someone who's never had love, never understood it, and who has fucked her way trying to find it. Every physical encounter is a distancing of the previous one, all the way back to the anguish

168

of remembering a world that you can never go back to. And I too, am looking back at that time, aching. Summers catching fireflies only to release them and watch them fly away, rolling down hills laughing and not caring about anything else, the sweater my grandma made me that smelled faintly like cinnamon, a time and place of endless possibilities. All this fucking... useless random fucking to feel that pinnacle, that climax of coming because it's the closest tangible facsimile of joy. And I'm seeing her there with me, in that far away nostalgic past, in the high of the present, and in an optimistic future... Two hearts numbing a tortured existence by burying loneliness in between the thighs of strangers, now opening up to let the other in.

"I still can't believe you can do that." She's texting to me.

"I know, right? You wouldn't think I'd be so perpetually single haha."

"Well you might not be anymore :)"

"Are you claiming me? :)"

"Damn right I am haha ;)" Heaven envelops me, that breathy dreamy consciousness filling my mind.

"So you don't mind me completely dominating your cunt like that?"

"Not at allll... In fact, I am very submissive, and love being dominated."

"I've always wanted a girl to surrender herself to me, totally. To let the pleasure overwhelm her, while simultaneously throbbing to please me." I take her panties out of my pocket. She slipped them in when we hugged, her scent is still on them. It's somehow a known, engrained scent, instinctually learned and sought out and it's raw and it's pure. "But I also want those days of you sitting on my face, smothering me and rubbing your pussy all over me and marking me as yours. And you know, cute cuddles and shit too haha :)"

170

"You're perfect. Look at this picture!" And I'm looking at a picture of her breasts, purple from severe bruising and aggressive groping.

"I don't want to see this :(" There's a blurring between inflicting pain and wanting to be in control, that I'll never be able to cross—certain things hurt you to your teeth to see. "I don't want to see you in pain, or know that you were with someone that was doing that to you."

"I'm sorry," she's saying, "I definitely didn't like it as much as with you. I thought with you saying you like dominance you might have liked that."

"Well, I don't think that's what true submission and dominance is. I think that's what someone would do as a shortcut to it. I think it's about each other surrendering, not just the sub but the Dom as well. So much psychological and physiological pleasure comes from me making you cum, and that you'll do anything I say without hesitation. It's like... I don't even need the act of you doing it, but the willingness. And I think the extreme violence just really isn't for me." A flash goes through my mind of my mom on the sidewalk with blood coming out of her head, when she fell when I was a kid... No, I tell it, go back into the abyss, as I thumb another Wellbutrin.

"I would love for you to tell me exactly what to do, and then to obey you."

"Obey you what?"

"Obey you... Sir."

"That's a good girl :)"

I am waiting for the day that I don't get a text from her, for it to be over and petered out like all the other passionate first dates in the past. But it never comes—right from the beginning we both knew we were equals, and we never question the obsessive consuming of the other. We're on the verge of a thousand texts within the first few weeks of us talking. There aren't any lows, or forced conversations about small talk, but it's as if we're on the same wavelength, and are just exchanging each other's day-to-day consciousness. The unproven optimism I've always wanted, is finally indisputable. I find myself entering rooms smiling, no longer merely just a beach house to be visited on a wild weekend once a year. There are as many non-sexual exchanges about work, life, goals, movies and so on, but it tends to always come back to making love, hard fucking, being tongue deep in her ass, and soft kisses on shoulders.

She's at a Starbucks, typing up a college paper. "This is just taking forever."

"Aw, you'd probably rather be with me huh? ;)"

"Definitely <3"

"I want you to go to the bathroom, and to touch yourself."

"But I'm here with people."

"Don't disobey me. Excuse yourself, then go to the bathroom, stick a finger inside your pussy, and then suck on it."

"Yes, master." A few minutes pass, and she texts me again. "I did it for you."

"Did it for me what?"

"I did it for you, Sir :)"

"And tell your master, did you like the way you taste?"

"Yes I did."

"That's a good girl :)"

"Mm, I love being your good girl :)"

Sushi Date

I'm driving with her, brimming with
happiness, a mutual love of sushi and lust for each
other on the horizon. I'm in jeans and a T-shirt,
she's wearing a skirt with no panties—dutifully
obeying my command. I'm rubbing her thigh with
my right hand as I'm driving, and she's looking at
me, blushing and furrowing her eyebrows in the
anguish and ecstasy. I'm keeping her right on the
edge, never getting her to peak, but her tongue is
hungrily finding its way down my throat at red
lights. I'm teasing her, asking her where to turn
right as I start to grab her chest, and she can't help
but moan and lose track of her thoughts. "What
was that, I didn't catch that?" I say, teasingly. And
when we arrive, I'm walking behind her, my hand
squeezing her from behind and rubbing her pussy
and ass at the same time. She calmly walks in, and
I slyly remove my hand, but not for long. I'm sitting
next to her, blocking off the other restaurant
patrons' view of my hand going up her skirt. She's

175

biting her lip, looking at me in love, my hand caressing her soaking thigh, inching ever closer to her clit until I can't bear to tease her any longer. My hand is rubbing her thigh up and down in such a way that each caress is secondarily massaging her clit with my pinky. She starts to tremble, and looks at me as if to say to stop.

"I can't believe I came and no one even knows. Did you see how jealous those girls looked to see me walk in with you?"

"So it wasn't just me feeling that?"

"No not at all, they're probably going to say what a bitch I am," and she lets out a giggle.

"So you don't think they know?"

"I think you hid it well, but if you kept going, I was going to get very loud."

I'm feeling as though I have pleased her enough, that I'm worthy and validated, and my physical arousal is lined up with my psychological arousal. She's putting me inside herself, in the hotel, and the warmth radiating out from her is overwhelming. Her pussy is soaking wet. It's not just the dinner, where I was fondling her only semi-privately, it's not just the walk down the hallway where the anticipation is building, and it's not just the kisses that I've been giving her that are the foreplay. The entirety of our lives have been building up to each other, every interaction and colossal failure and fleeting happiness brought us to this exact point, our entire existence a flirtation with this moment where we're not just fucking, not even making love, but instead are two people combining as one for an instant of pure happiness. Pure joy. I'm close to cumming, the warmth and tightness are too much. I'm telling her that I'm going to cum, and she pulls me out and sucks my cock until I cum in her mouth. She lies next to me, and after multiple orgasms we are our unblemished selves. "We should go get ice cream," she's saying. Her words are so light and bubbly that I'm unable to resist, and I don't even mention my dairy allergy. When we get back from the store, she finds a site to stream *Hotel Hell*, and I'm asking her how she was able to find it online so easily. She just giggles and says it's easy. We're eating the ice cream while watching TV, and it's a surreal feeling—all these unknown places after sex.

Morning comes. We both wake at the same time, as if we share a dream rapport. We're getting in the shower, and I'm behind her letting her have the hot water. I'm lathering her hair with the Dove shampoo and conditioner that I bought to use on her, meticulously soaping each of her curls, letting my fingers linger through her scalp, massaging softly. Her shoulders only slightly slope forward because of her large chest, which I'm now caressing, admiring the blue veins which show through her porcelain skin—an entire universe of processes and living organisms pulsating within her. And it's dawning on me as I touch her that I'm touching divinity, and that the most miraculous thing is that we're both here next to each other when we could have been anyone else, anywhere else in the world. I'm alive, I'm breathing air that has particles in it from eons ago, and I'm experiencing a miracle at my fingertips.

Those Three Little Words

Our goodbyes are getting progressively harder, and I'm already feeling a longing to be near her again as I'm driving away. There's a house, more like a hunter's shack, off to the side of the highway, only about 20 minutes away from her. I find it online, and the pictures are only of the outside, but I can imagine the inside. I see a hole in the ceiling that needs to be repaired so that water doesn't leak in on rainy days. I see moldy walls that need torn out, and that new, thicker insulation needs to be installed. A kerosene heater is off to the side, but I would put in a pellet stove. It isn't much, but with her, it would be more than enough. I keep the idea in the back of my mind, waiting until the next time I see her to tell her, but even the idea itself gives me enough comfort to assuage the longing.

I'm driving back to her house for our next date, frustrated at how slow the traffic is moving, and I'm passing a truck when I hear the distinct siren wail of a cop. He's going through the motions of the power dynamics, and all I'm thinking of is that he's keeping me from Sabrina.

"I had you going 75 in a 55."

"That's bullshit man, I was speeding I'll give you that, but I wasn't going 75. I was going 60, max." Maybe it's the certainty of the statement, or that I legitimately don't care about being pulled over, but he agrees with me after a while, and reduces my ticket to not have points. I keep speeding the rest of the way, texting her along the way about getting pulled over.

"It's okay that you're a little behind, I'm still getting ready ;)" She's half scolding me in the car, "I can't believe you got a speeding ticket, you should drive slower I'm fine waiting." We arrive again at the Stevens, and I practically kick the door down. I'm throwing her on the bed. I start spanking her hard, and she whimpers at first, then coos and moans in delight. I'm yanking her pants down, savagely, exposing her perfect ass and spreading her cheeks and start tonguing her asshole deeply. I don't build to it, or tease it, I'm just there licking it in all its forbidden glory.

"Get on your knees." I command to her, holding both her hands above her head, and she's dutifully complying. My pants are down, my cock in her face, and I start thrusting into her adorable mouth, fucking her face hard. "You belong to me, you're my property" I'm saying, thrusting harder. "Now you say it."

With my cock throbbing on the side of her face, she says "I belong to you, I'm your property" while gasping for air, and I shove my cock back inside her. I'm feeling a tremble coming from her that's not unlike an orgasm. I take her back to the bed, and affectionately start to lick and suckle her clit while fingering her. She's cumming already, after only a few moments of licking. I'm holding her down, fucking her as hard as I want, and she's loving every second of it. She's riding me now. It's

182

too much and I'm pulling out to cum on her face, which she encourages me to take a picture of.

While I'm recovering, I start to finger fuck her very roughly and she's squirting everywhere again. I notice a little blood on the bed, and I worry that I've been too rough, but she's really enjoying it, and doesn't want me to stop when I bring it up. I'm starting to say to her "release yourself to me" in an intimate whisper, as I look deeply into her eyes, and she knows that I'm saying to let herself be truly naked. She cums harder than I have ever seen a person, in real life or in porn, and something transformative is happening. She's no longer confined to the limitations of a traditional orgasm. I've finally done it—I've found that special person who would let down all her barriers. All the thousands of nerve endings associated with her clitoris start radiating over the whole of her body, and everything is beyond an erogenous zone. I'm seeing this change take place, knowing that this is a shared experience that few will ever know, and I revel in its power. I start kissing her belly button, licking it, and she cums. I'm suckling her nipples, and even more wetness builds on the bed from her orgasm. A trace of my fingertip across her shoulder, and she's convulsing with pleasure.

"What are you doing to me?" She asks, somewhat concerned, and my fingers trace down her thigh and she twitches and cums again.

"It's something I've wanted to have happen for a long time. I've always thought that it just required a girl being relaxed and open enough to let me sort of turn on this orgasm 'switch'."

"You're perfect."

"Yeah? You don't want to be with anyone else?"

"Never." My hand grabs her pussy, and I'm giving her a soft kiss on the lips. I'm tired, and she's running her fingertips through my chest hair, and I'm still gently rubbing her shoulder and making her shiver with little orgasms. *The Tonight*

184

Show with Jimmy Fallon comes on, with Gordon Ramsey as a guest. I'm watching, and I say to her that I want her to touch herself to Gordon, but not to Jimmy, and she laughs about the specification. I start choking her, as she's rubbing her clit watching the interview, and she cums again. After lying there for a while, she says softly, "I love you." I start to smile, but before I respond she quickly says "I'm sorry I just say that to everyone I know, I don't mean to be weird."

"It's okay, I love you too." I say this with sincerity, whether or not she cares to admit that it was something more than an aloof casual statement on her part. One only needs a spark to burn, and a name becomes an opulent palace in the mind. We're two fallen angels, who have both been disfigured through life, but who are beautiful once again in the other's presence. I'm telling her in my roundabout way about the little shack, and she's saying that it sounds nice, but that she doesn't want me to spend any money. Everything feels all right, as though I've finally arrived at a destination I've been moving towards my entire life. Even the air feels different—lighter somehow, and I need to take deeper and more frequent breaths, lest I get lightheaded.

We're going down the aisle of a Whole Foods. "You have to try cookie butter," she's saying, an ear-to-ear grin on her face. Someone is there with sample spoons.

"Oh my god yes, this is amazing!" I'm making genuine "mmm" and "oh god yes" noises, to which she says, "adorable," and keeps smiling. "I want to go to a bed and breakfast with you one weekend. I hate having to say goodbye, and I want to be selfish and have you longer. It'll be a weekend filled with cuddles and movies, and cookie butter of course."

"I'd like that a lot, but I don't know about the money."

"Oh hush, it's nothing." Her arm is

encircling mine, her rosy cheek resting on my shoulder, and my muscles tighten at first to her delight, then relax. "I just think you're so sweet and adorable, and you mean a lot to me, and I care for you."

"I like you too, I just... I don't know."

"What's wrong?" There's distance in her voice.

"Sometimes I worry that I don't have the emotions that other people do. Like you're really amazing, and so nice to me, but I don't know if I'm good enough for you. I feel like I don't deserve you."

"Well of course you deserve me, and I've seen that you care. I think there's an entire world of feelings inside you that you've just had to put away, because other guys have been so bad to you. And now you have this barrier, that's trying to keep me out from those feelings to protect you. It doesn't always have to be bad." And I smile, sincerely at her, and kiss her on the cheek.

"You might be right, and I know you're a great guy. I'm sorry."

"Hush," I say affectionately, "you don't have anything to be sorry for."

Later that night she's texting me, "Hey, do you have SnapChat?"

"No, isn't that mostly for dick pics? Haha, I don't have much use for it, I prefer texting."

"Well you should get it, because I look cute and want you to see throughout your day. :)"

"Well alright, if you're going to twist my arm :p" She's sending me pictures of her wearing the new scarf that I got her, and her cheeks are rosy from a run in the early winter morning. And just like that, it vanishes after the 10 second delay, as if to say that none of the romance of this new world is designed to last. I think about the first photographs that took several minutes to capture, and I realize that we've come so far that we can easily capture little fragments of memories, and that we casually squander these moments on a temporary medium—nothing more than a passing "hello" to a stranger. But my days are better by receiving them, and I'm happy to be involved in her life.

In the following days, she's been very sick with a cold, and I decide that I want to prepare her a lasagna, her favorite dish. I also want to further our roleplaying, and I'm buying a pink collar and leash for her. I take great pleasure in checking out at the pet store, the clerk asking me about the breed of dog, going over the pros and cons of collars, never knowing that this was for a person. I text her a picture of me tightly clutching the leash and collar. "Oh my god, it's so cute! You're too good to me, Master. I was thinking of buying a pair of vibrating panties with a remote controller that you could... use on me in a restaurant. And I'd have to try to not to cum too loudly :)"

"I dunno, I think I'd like it a lot more if we

bought it together and looked at all the toys :)"

"Okay! I just wish I wasn't so sick though :("

"I wish you'd let me take care of you. I can make you a soup or get oranges to squeeze some juice for you. Or my muscly arms can give you massages :)"

"Uggh I want all those things, but I'm really sick."

"Okay, well maybe you should go to the doctor then, honey."

"I know I know, I'm going in a few days."

"Okay honey. Oh also, I think we need to involve this too ;)" And I attach another picture of me, I'm shopping at Wal-Mart, grabbing a bunch of rope and clutching it even tighter than I was her leash.

"Uggh rope too? I want it so bad! I wish I felt better!"

"All right, no more teasing from me. I hope

you feel better :)" I'm getting more out of my
workouts in the gym, work feels like it's not work,
and every room I enter feels like I'm conquering it.
I'm in love and life makes sense again.

In My Pocket

I'm running low on Wellbutrin, and I'm calmly calling my doctor to schedule a refill—only to discover that she's no longer practicing. I'm re-reading the warnings that came with my prescription, and the phrase "suicidal thoughts" keeps looping in my mind. I flash back to driving on the highway, years ago, letting go of the steering wheel... I'm telling Sabrina about needing a prescription, and we talk at length about her also being on medication, and she tells me that she's not doing well with it. Maybe this crutch can be left behind, the new love stitching up those wounds. I know I'm not quite strong enough to quit cold turkey, so I call up a new practice only to discover they aren't taking new patients.

"See here's the thing, I'm going to just be honest with you. I'm just worried about... the side effects of getting off an anti-depressant." I'm starting to choke up "Like, you know depressing thoughts, or you know, something awful like

192

suicide."

"We can maybe see you in a couple of months, but right now it's very tight." I think about Sabrina again, wrapping around me at the mere mention of the word "tight." I'm explaining my predicament to the pharmacist at Wal-Mart, and I'm getting emotional. He gives me, with whatever extenuating circumstances power he has, an emergency refill for four more days of Wellbutrin. I look in his eyes with gratitude, and see the best of humanity helping me in his eyes. I make another trip to the Urgent Care center, hoping to get at least one more prescription. I'm getting nervous around the sick people, wishing that this was all over already. I'm called in to a room, and in a surreal moment, it's the same doctor that worked on my big toe. He's still astutely looking down his glasses, which fall partway down his nose.

"Okay, so what brings you in today?" He's looking straight at me, a look he's given a thousand junkies before, watching for lies.

"Well uh, it's just that my doctor, who I usually see for my refills of Wellbutrin, apparently she's no longer practicing. And well, I'm just honestly really worried about getting off of it, and I know you know." I'm aware I'm saying "you know" nervously, as I usually do in anxious situations. "Well I, you know, I don't want to hurt myself over it." Please, with everything inside you, give me three months, that's all I'll need I swear. "I decided that I want to stop taking it, but that I just want a couple months to lower my dosage. So I was hoping for a month of my regular dosage, and then a month at a lower dosage, like half or so."

"I'm going to give you one month of your dosage. That's being generous. I normally only give two weeks, and then have a follow up. I recommend a follow up to see where you're at and to evaluate you." He's so professional, so textbook—there is no unearned pity.

"Well I appreciate it, I do." The bill is too much for me to keep going, so I start thinking long term and when I get home, I start splitting my pills into halves. I take one half in the morning, and keep one half in my pocket to take at night, and this alone doubles my prescription and my chances. I'm telling Sabrina all this, and asking her when I'll see her again.

"I don't know, I still don't feel well."

"Aw, you still don't feel good? That's it, I'm coming up to you and I'm bringing you soup and we're going to snuggle and fuck each other's brains out until you feel all better :)"

"Ugh that sounds amazing, but I would feel terrible if I got you sick."

"I don't mind, it's fine!"

"No really, I would hate myself if I got you sick."

"Okay, well, yeah you're probably right. I'm going to go to the gym, then. Send me a picture to motivate me ;)" I'm looking at the picture of her perfect breasts, nipples cold and hard as she lies in her bed, and I'm asking her how badly she needs them sucked on. I'm remembering making her cum by licking them, and I'm remembering her soft tongue in her mouth—unsure but wanting—and I'm remembering her moaning. While on the way to the gym, my hand unconsciously rubs against my cock, even after jerking off at home. My daydreams must've gotten the best of me, as I have pre-cum oozing out as I go to take a piss at the urinal. I'm working bench today, planning on going especially hard, and in between sets I look at her pictures again. I'm feeling her hands admiring my chest and arms and shoulders again as soon as she's better—my paradise.

Our power dynamics are evolving, as she now feels compelled to ask my permission to touch herself, and I revel in this. "I think I might have to make a paddle for you, for when you disobey <3" I say, because she started to touch herself without asking.

"Yes yesss you should do that."

"Have you been home? Why have you not been begging today?! :P"

"I'm so high I got really distracted. I will after I make this English muffin."

"Haha, you are so adorable I love it <3"

"<333"

"Know what's really amazing?? English muffin pizzas!"

"Oh my god I need one," she says, and I can picture taking care of her, nourishing her in a way she likely has never been nourished. Putting love into every action, even the most basic actions. "Or like 3."

"I can make you some! I just love making you happy, and I have to keep my sub happy and feeling loved <3"

"That's so nice. Can I touch myself now please??"

"You haven't been begging at all tonight! So start begging :)"

"Pllleeaase <3 <3"

"No, you need to think about pleasing me more. Describe it to me, how you love pleasing me, and how wet it makes you."

"I love pleasing you, especially when you fuck my mouth, and I love swallowing your cum <3 it makes me sooo wet." I couldn't be more in love.

"Do you feel like a good girl when I fuck your face?"

"Mhmm <3"

"Is it like overwhelming when I make you cum? Start squeezing your breasts <3"

"Yes, that's the perfect word."

"I want you to start tracing your fingers over your hips, and tell me—are you soaking through your panties?"

"Yes, master." "Yes!"

198

"Squeeze your pussy over your panties."

"I can feel my clit throbbing <3" I'm starting to ache as well, her building pleasure increasing my satisfaction, and even though we're only texting, we're being more intimate than most people who are in the same room usually are.

"Picture the release of touching your clit, the building orgasm, the tremble in your body, but only brush up against it over your panties. And when you've done that, and it feels like you can't handle it, I want you to take your panties off and caress your pussy lightly. Not in a way that would make you cum, but in an affectionate way to your clit."

"Mmm, oh my Godd."

"Thank me for my kindness, then touch yourself, and really let go with how hard you cum, and cum for me <3"

"Thank you so much, I did!" A few minutes pass and she adds, "Twice <3" Her perfect little clitoris that I love is the epitome of perfection, a thing of reverence in it's divinity and every one of it's 8,000 nerve endings—the pinnacle of evolution.

"Aren't you glad you found such a kind master?"

"Yes, so glad. And you should definitely make a paddle for me when I'm bad ;)"

"My hands will do fine for now, they're very strong ;) Plus, you're a good girl more often than not. I definitely would've spanked you hard today though, for no real reason either."

"You can on Thursday! Please do on Thursday, when I'm wearing my collar."

"And when I do spank you, very hard, and your ass is sore and red, I'm going to gently caress it, and ease my finger in to your asshole—and you are to thank me <3"

"Yes please master <3 Can I maybe touch myself again?"

"Tell me how amazing it feels when I tongue and finger your asshole."

"I love it sooo much, it feels amazing."

"And you're glad I showed you this new pleasure?"

"Yes! Thank you for showing me master."

"You're grateful to have your asshole owned and pleasured by me? To do with as I please?"

"Yes! Thank you for showing me master. Should I finger it?"

"As deep as your finger will go :)"

"Yes, master."

"Think about my cock being in there, massaging your G-spot, throbbing inside you. And how grateful you would be that your body serves my need for pleasure."

"I would be so grateful."

"Is that because everything about you belongs to me? Repeat what we both know to be the absolute truth."

"Everything on me belongs to you. I belong to you."

"I want you to finger your ass, while fingering your pussy with your other hand, and to massage your clit with your palm while you finger yourself. Do that until it's unbearable, then make yourself cum for me <3"

"Thank you!"

After some time passes, I tell her that my phone is acting funny. I probably have a virus or need to delete some pictures, because I hoard every picture that a girl has ever sent me or has put on a dating profile. "Get some rest, my beautiful pet <3"

"I love you master! Goodnight!"

Out of Control

"I have some good news!" She texts me, the next day, clearly overjoyed.

"Are you finally feeling all better? :)"

"Well I am better, but I got a new job! I'm going to be a hostess at a bar/restaurant."

"That's fucking great! Now you can finally save up for a car haha :)"

"Nooo, not yet haha."

"Ahh well, I'm proud. I know you didn't like your other job."

"I fucking hated it haha."

"Haha, so what are you going to tell all those poor guys that try and hit on you?"

There's what feels like a lifetime of a pause in between our texts, and then, "I don't know" is her response.

"Well what do you mean? You're my

property."

"Yes, master, I am. I just, I don't know, I think I'm not good enough for you."

"This again? Come on, we've been over this already."

"I just think, I mean, I like being with you, and the sex is amazing. I just think it might be better for me at my job if I don't say I'm with someone."

"You mean for tips?"

"Yeah. I can't be in a relationship right now." And with so few words, my world is shattered.

"But you're exclusive to me right now with sex?"

"Or like, in the foreseeable future." Our texts are a little out of sync. "Yeah but I can't—"

"I'm fine if you don't want to be in a relationship. I know you have feelings issues. Just let me know when you're maybe wanting to have sex with someone else. I just... don't want it to happen without me knowing."

"—do this thing that we've been doing."

"And I really want to see you more than once a week, but you make it out like you can't." I can hardly see the screen on my phone. I'm on the verge of a nervous breakdown, and my eyes are too watery.

"Like I caaan't at all, I'm sorry. I just don't have room for this in my life, and we are at completely different parts of life, and have different goals and dreams, and I just need to focus on myself. Nooo, that's not ok with me."

"Do you want to see me Thursday?"

"I feel so bad, but I can't let this go further than it has. And you're like, the nicest and sweetest person ever, and also you can make me cum again and again, and I'll probably never find someone as great as you, but I feel like an awful person for not being as emotionally invested as you. And I don't wanna do it anymore. I... do wanna see you, but I can't. You have to understand how different our lives are... Like, age isn't a problem for me, but us being at very different stages of life is a problem."

But it's already gone too far. I'm in love with you and have been for a while, and it's all spiraled predictably out of control. It's all I've known—to chase that intensity. And in the process, I have fallen into the familiar pitfall of modern alchemy, trying to turn casual sex into true love. I understand more than she realizes. I know that she actually does care even though it was supposed to be casual, and it scares the hell out of her. And I know that this presents itself to her as things like marriage and kids, and that she assumes that's where I am, too. I'm wanting to tell her all this, that it's okay, and I don't know how. "One last night of pure, unattached, good sex? I would be okay with that."

"I can't... I feel too bad... I didn't even plan on doing this right now, it just happened."

"If you want to see me, then see me. I would be much better with that than this." I'm cradling my phone, hoping for a yes.

"I know I'm horrible. I'm sorry, it's just not what I need right now. I need to focus on like, figuring my life and myself out, and that's something you have to do by yourself."

"I disagree, but I won't stop you. I really wish you would've waited to tell me in person."

"I couldn't wait. I'm really sorry, but you deserve and will have better than me, anyway. I feel really bad, and I'm probably going to regret this very soon, but I had to do it."

"No, you don't need to do that. I've been dumped plenty of times, and nothing you say can make it easier. I do have something else to say." I don't want this to be any more difficult for her, and I'm trying to offer her advice in the wreckage of my defeat. "I want to thank you, for being understanding of my desire to please so much. And I want to thank you, for doing something wonderful for me, because now we both at least have an idea of what a relationship is like. And for that, I do sincerely love you, and always will, probably... I was on the verge of doing the most wonderful things for you... Getting a better job to help you get a car, and to be able to spend each weekend with you. I know we're two people who both know in their heart of hearts that we belong together, even if one of us is a bit of a commitaphobe because she's still terrified that she'll end up hurt again. Keep my memory, and the gifts I gave you as a gentle reminder, that you can have good things. That there are good people out there. And when you find them, don't be like me and be a pussy about it. Because as I was trying to tell you before, feelings can be the greatest and most exhilarating things you can encounter, if you let them happen. My number will remain the same, and I'm here if you want to rekindle the flame. I will remember the sex, and the dirty talk, but that won't be what I take from this. It's the closeness, waking up next to you, and holding you tight. At least now you know what you deserve. You're young, and maybe all you know how to do is run away, like I did countless times. I won't hold it against you. I hope you find your way, and please be careful with guys. I can't bear the thought of you being hurt ever again. Take care, and you know where to find me lovely <3" I set my phone down, and I writhe in anguish. I don't know where I'll be in a month—if all those memories and life will drown me and overwhelm me again. I'm walking into the bathroom, staggering there, throwing up in the hallway from coughing and crying.

It's the next day and I'm looking at a brunette girl while I'm at work. She seems vaguely familiar, and she's looking at me strangely. It's this girl Sarah, who I invited to my trailer a year or two ago and ate her pussy endlessly while *A Nightmare on Elm Street* played softly in the background because she said she liked horror movies. She pretends to not recognize me, doesn't want to strike up a conversation because she's gained weight since I last saw her. I oblige her unspoken request, and go through the motions at work. I get a text late that night after work, from Sabrina. "I miss you and I don't know what to do about this. Should I just ignore it until it goes away? I don't know anything."

"You could do that, or just be with me. I mean, you could just write off yesterday as bipolar-ness if you want." Patients used to be bled nearly to death, and this was thought to remedy all ailments.

"I would ignore me if I were you. You should probably ignore me." She's probably drunk or high, but I like to think that she just misses me as much as I miss her.

210

"Nah, I wouldn't. And you know, the times I let feelings just fade away were awful, and I wouldn't wish you to do that. It's brutal. The only problem is I cancelled the motel earlier. I always want to see you though."

"I know I wasn't asking you to see me... I just don't know what to do."

"Well, would you want to see me?" I just know I could win her over, and that my burning love and endless orgasms would make her fall in love with me again.

"I do, but I can't just do this to you. You don't deserve me just yanking you around, and I don't mean to, I'm just like... I just don't know how I feel. And I don't know if I'm in this relationship for just the perks."

"Do you mean to say that you really like the sex, but you're unsure about liking me?"

"That sounds mean. I like you, I just don't know what that means to me."

"But isn't that just because you've been bouncing around with guys that you're used to abandoning you or hurting you?"

"I don't know why it is. This is why I feel like it won't work. You just have more life experiences, and you have everything figured out more than I do... You want different things than me I think! Like really serious things that are scary to me. Am I being dumb? I don't know what to do. Tell me exactly what to do. I can't make decisions. I just want someone else to make all my decisions for me forever, because I'm obviously not equipped to do it myself. I hate myself."

"I think you should call the hotel tonight, and ask for a room on Thursday. Then I want you to put all these negative thoughts out of your head, about hating yourself and thinking you're a bad person. Then I want you to go to bed, and get a good night's sleep. And when Thursday comes, I want you to relax, smoke a bowl and ease your mind, and stay the night with me, and realize this

212

all was silly. But most importantly, I want you to not hate yourself. There is a good person somewhere inside you."

"I'm 99% sure there is not a good person anywhere inside of me lol. I hate myself and everything about myself, like an irreversible amount, and I think I always will, which is another reason I don't think I can do a relationship."

"Do you want to see me or not that day?"

"I don't want to take advantage of you."

"It's yes or no. Do you want to suck my cock?"

"Ugh, yess"

"Do you want to fuck me, and to be drinking my cum?"

"Mhmm."

"You won't cancel if I get a room?"

"I want to see you, and I won't cancel, and I will suck your cock alll night. Ugh, I just don't know if I can have my life be complicated by a relationship right now, when so much else is going on. I can't like commit to anything, not even a non-commitment thing." There's a pause in between her texts, and she continues being painfully honest. "I cried all day because I didn't have anything to wear, and I hate myself. I can't really even stand the sight of myself today."

"Why?"

"I'm sorry :("

"Why are you so damn hard on yourself?"

"I'm not, I just can't look at myself today because it horrifies and disgusts me. I just hate myself."

"You aren't allowed to hate yourself anymore. You said that you want someone to make your decisions for you, so there, I made that one for you :)"

"Hahaha that's not even a decision though,

it's just who I am. I'm sorry! We should probably say goodbye on Thursday... if you still want to."

"Do you want me to fuck your asshole, with you tied up?"

"Yesss"

"Say it."

"Please fuck my asshole with me tied up."

"You'll suck it clean, too."

"Mhmm." This will only make things worse, and harder to pull away if I need to, but I want it all the same because I want it to work. I want to be the thing that heals her, and for her to heal me, because I never knew how to put the work in on myself. "Okay, no I was wrong, I keep making mistakes. I can't, I can't."

"What were you wrong about?"

"I'm better off alone. I have to be alone. Don't think that I don't want to be with you, I just should be alone. Everything, always. I'm sorry, I should have left things all clean. I made them messy again. This is what happens when I don't get high for one day. I should have just gotten high and gone to sleep. I'm sorry, I'm sorry. I'm sorry for not being able to do this."

"It's okay. I don't blame you." I thought of her as the one throwing me a lifeline in the storm of life, but the reality is that we're both drowning in the same ocean of sadness. And I'm accepting that she, for as dutiful of a submissive as she was for me and as strict of a master as I was for her, won't let me tell her what to do this time. Another girl is texting me. She's at a bar and she's telling me how she's thinking about all the times her boyfriend isn't around to satisfy her. It could be anyone else in the bar who takes her home to fuck her, who could provide the overwhelming thrill to quiet her boredom, and instead she chooses me. I'm too heartbroken, from being dumped for the second time by the same person, and I'm turning her down because of it. If only it had been a few days later, if only "Love Me Harder" by Ariana Grande wasn't on the radio on my late-night aimless drive, and if only I wasn't feeling the memory of Sabrina's hips grinding on mine. The window of opportunity closes, on the girl in the bar, and even though I want to fuck her, I'm relieved it doesn't happen.

I'm gorging on sushi the next day, eating way too much. I'm full, but I continue to eat, a leftover form of punishing myself from when I was a fat kid... Just keep on numbing everything... "I want you in between my legs right now," a girl named Kaitlin is texting me, another case of terrible timing.

"Oh man, I'm so full of sushi right now. I don't even think I can move."

"I don't even care, I'll just ride you and fuck you."

"Oh jeez, I think any movement and I'll barf haha. Can I get a rain check? I'll very gladly come lick you endlessly and fuck your brains out another night :)"

"I am so horny I don't even think I would mind, just get over here."

Because I haven't had enough emotional masochism, I'm texting her "What's your address?" I pay my bill, and with labored breathing, I carefully walk to my car. I'm driving, and I manage to get about half a mile away from the restaurant, and my body rejects the amount of food I ate. There's particles of squid and tuna on my dash, in my automatic locks, on my shirt, and I'm crying. I'm so far away from that night with Sabrina getting sushi... I fall asleep in my car for a few minutes out of exhaustion. I use a shirt that's laying in my back seat to clean up most of the mess, and drive home.

I'm at the gym the next day, checking out the high school seniors using the oblique machine, and I duck into the bathroom because I feel myself getting hard. Thankfully, it goes away and I'm taking a piss, noticing a lot of pre-cum oozing out of my cock. It must be a result of getting older. I start doing pullups in front of the girls, really controlling my form and hoping they notice my arms and back. I'm flexing in the mirror, as if it's only for myself. I've been in the gym for too long, and I'm too hungry to think straight, so I leave to get food. I'm getting a burrito bowl and saying, "Give me an amount of sriracha that like, you'd be concerned about giving me." I'm pounding my fist on the table and my sinuses are opening up, and later when I'm at home taking a piss, I'm regretting the amount of sriracha I ate, as it burns when I'm pissing. The next day at work, I'm in the bathroom taking a piss. More cum is on my leg, and there's a deep ache when I'm pissing. I'm thinking that it must be blue balls again. The thought keeps gnawing at me—what could it be? It's not until later that I'm jerking off, and I cum thick stringy knotted ropes of jizz, that my power of denial is diminished. I'm doing a Google search for "what could it mean when a girl is spotting" thinking back to the last time I was with Sabrina... Chlamydia comes up, and statistics that 75% of females will exhibit no symptoms, and that younger girls are more likely to be prone to STD's, and that it takes three weeks to manifest. It's been that long since I've been with Sabrina... and still I'm bargaining it's a UTI.

Testing

I'm sitting in the too cozy waiting room of a Christian pregnancy and STD clinic. There are only two rooms—the bigger pregnancy room, and the unmarked, hidden STD room. A happy couple sits across from me, and I'm trying to not make eye contact while filling out the forms alone. They both know why I'm here, and they can't mask their unconscious judgement of me. I'm relieved when I'm called back, and a younger woman with a clipboard starts to interview me. She asks me what made me come in, in a way that's politely asking if I sleep around a lot.

"Well you know, I just sort of find myself in these situations where girls just want a physical thing. I don't go in to it with that in mind—well some of the times, maybe—but usually I just go along with what they want, because I hope it leads to a relationship."

"That's so interesting. The females I

normally talk with in here always say that they only go along with what the guy wants."

"No way. They decided before even spending time with those guys that they wanted to have sex with them. Most people get dates out of the way with texting these days, so they feel less guilty about hooking up on the first date. I'm not saying I'm completely innocent, but those girls just want to make it seem like it wasn't fully their decision. Girls have all the power."

"And, have you been with a lot of partners?" She's playing with a ring on a necklace, and her hips have relaxed ever so slightly. She's allowing herself to forget her strong moral code and her marriage, and to enjoy my confessions in just the slightest way.

"Well, I probably average about two or three a year, because when I find someone, I stick with them, even though it usually turns out that I'm the other guy, or that I'm being cheated on. I don't always go all the way, but a lot of kissing and oral sex is involved. It's much more intimate I think."

"Well there are still risks with that, of course." She's looking in the direction of the pamphlets in front of me, and I'm looking up her skirt slightly and wondering if she has fine tufts of bush there, if it would be too naughty to her to shave her pussy. I'm thinking about how I would make her cum while breathing in that veritable forest of purity.

"I know, I know. I want to be good. I want to be good and in a relationship with one partner. It's so... hard anymore to get your foot in the door."

"What do you mean? I'm just curious because I haven't dated in so long, and I met my husband through my church."

"Well as a guy, you have to accept that you're just one of a hundred guys a girl could be with, and it doesn't work the other way. A guy might have four or five girls interested in him, unless he's super attractive or something. So you have this tiny window of opportunity as it is, and if you're funny and charming, then great, right? Well, if you're funny, charming, smart, kind, and all these other qualities in real life, then sure. But you have to now be all those things, plus be attentive while also being hard to get, have that sweet side but pretty much never show it, be sexy but walk the line between being overtly sexy when they want it and then forgetting about it until they bring it up, and be confident and everything else all through texting. It's exhausting. It's almost as if texting is a new skill that somehow signals to them that you have these qualities. And that's not even the worst of it. You have to also most likely, have a degree of some sort, even though that's completely arbitrary and shows only a willingness to indebt yourself for a pretentious piece of paper. I know that the subtext is that it shows good job security, and I mean, yeah, obviously doctors and

224

crap need that, but you get what I'm saying." She's nodding her head in understanding. "You also have to know exactly who you are, where you are in life, where you want to go in life, and have everything regimented and planned to a T and hope that it lines up with their goals, while also being able to be spontaneous and willing to go on long random drives and the like. And the really fucked up thing, is that I am all of those things! But the reality is, for a lot of people, they make this idea of a perfect person. They have this checklist of qualities, and they tend to reject someone if they don't have all these qualities. And a lot of it, is to not only continue to be alone, but to legitimize their belief that 'guys only want one thing' and such I guess for sympathy, instead of just running with it with someone they like."

"I can say I'm glad I'm married, because that sounds awful. Maybe you should take some time to yourself, and stop looking for it for a while?" As cliché advice as this is, she's probably right, but it

225

feels impossible, and I'm anxiously feeling my phone in my pocket, anticipating going on OkCupid after I leave.

"You're probably right... So if this ends up being that I have it... I should definitely call her up and let her know?"

"Well, we definitely want to hope for it to come back negative, but if it does go the other way, then yes, you will want to get in contact. And I know that can be awkward, and not what you want to do, but you really have to."

"Oh I definitely will. I would feel too terrible not to." I'm standing in the bathroom, holding the cup and telling myself to go, and I just can't do it. I can't let go. If this is in fact chlamydia, then it's from her and there's a part of her inside me, and I can't fucking let her go. I'm here long enough for the woman to sweetly knock on the door, asking softly if I'm okay. "I'm okay, I'm just nervous I think." Tiny painful spurts and drops come out and mostly I'm going on the floor, dribbling out of myself, and I'm hoping that I have enough in the cup as I leave. I'm in my car, fondling my half tablet of Wellbutrin, convincing myself to keep it together.

I'm at home sitting down, writing out a text to Sabrina, trying not to get too worked up, like when I was a kid and I would find myself hyperventilating. "So, this is awkward, and there's literally a hundred other things I would rather text you about. I was actually planning on texting you in a few weeks. But, I care too much for you not to tell you this. I don't mean to alarm you, but about five days ago, I noticed some burning when I peed. It was too inconsistent to think anything of it. But it got worse, and I did some reading. I think I just have a UTI, but I went for an STD test for chlamydia. You're the only one I've been with in the last few months. From what I read, there could be zero symptoms from either person, or it could be the same symptoms as a UTI. I'm not telling you this out of anger, or to worry you, but because I don't want you to be sick :((I will let you know how the test goes, but I just wanted to text you sooner rather than later, because you know I care so deeply for you. Not only do I not want you to also have to send out this awkward text, but I also don't want you to have something and not know it. So if you think you had/have a UTI, then get checked out, and if it turns out the other way, I'll let you know as soon as possible. And I also hope you're doing well, and that you're happy."

She responds quickly, "1, I have no symptoms. 2, I got tested weeks ago just because."

"Okay, well I'm glad. I wasn't implying anything about you, I just don't want to be shitty and not ever say anything one way or the other. And... don't think me not talking to you means I don't miss you—because I do, so much, every day. Not a second goes by without me wanting to hold you." I can't find my breath, and the nostalgia is overwhelming.

228

"I'm sorry."

"It's okay, honey, I know you had your reasons, and it was difficult for you too. I just don't want you getting the wrong idea, like I forgot you or don't like you, because that would be impossible. I just was trying to do what you wanted. Take care." I'm crying, scared out of my mind, but horny all the same. I've turned off the TV, and I'm sitting in silence. This is the most alone I've ever felt. I'm looking at porn on my phone out of habit, comforted in a way by the vicarious presence of the performers, but it's just not doing anything for me. I'm starting to touch myself, but I'm filled with despondency and with all my effort nothing happens. A part of me is wishing that I could somehow find them, and love them.

I'm filled with gratitude when my phone illuminates. It's Sabrina again. "How have you been doing? Unless you don't want to talk, which is totally fine."

"I'm okay," I lie. "I'm just anxious until I get the results of this test, and I've had endless caffeine so I crashed super hard and got depressed, and then crazy horny."

"Well that's not good. Sorry you had a bad day."

"Can I be blunt with you though?"

"Of course."

"I really wish I had you in a room right now, completely tied up and forcing you to suck my dick endlessly. For hours."

"Hahaha don't tempt me, you know how badly I wanna be tied up."

"Like right at the base of a bed, down on your knees, arms stretched out and tied behind you, and you just sucking away over and over and over."

"Ughhh"

"I know I just made your pussy wet, didn't

I?" I want to be close to her again, to actually love her as a person, and not be alone, and this is as close as I can get.

"Very."

"Taste it. I'm swollen and aching with how hard I am. And think about me licking your ass, and how great it feels."

"I did, mhmm."

"Torture yourself with the thought of you gushing from my touch, and then tell me how hungry you are for my cum."

"I'm soo hungry for your cum." I text her a picture of my cock and I'm telling her it belongs in her mouth, and tell her to show me what belongs in mine. She sends me a picture of her perfectly smooth pussy.

"Are you aching yet?"

"Yes, throbbing."

"Tease your clit, thrust your hips in the air

after you touch it, think about my cock inside you, and make that throbbing worse and worse by gently touching yourself. And beg for my finger in your asshole."

"Please, please, please put your finger in my ass while you fuck me." I'm starting to cum, that light-headed, about to pass out kind of orgasm. It comes out thick, and almost painful, like it was the first time.

"Good girl, now you know you can cum."

"Thank you, Sir."

"Thank you who?"

"Master*"

I'm marveling at my control of her, and how much I've missed it becomes obvious. "We ARE going to fuck in the future again, if you didn't already know. It's too good not to. I don't want anyone else any time soon. It doesn't matter if it's just once or a hundred times, it needs to happen again. Say you know you will be dominated again by me, that you crave it, need it."

"I know I'll be dominated by you again, I crave it and need it ;)" And just like that, it is really over. I would give anything to not have this be my last conversation with her, to be the man I'd always seen myself as. To tell her something deep—that an average person has 2.5 billion heartbeats in a lifetime. That I've had a billion heartbeats, every single one of them drawing me to her, and that she has every right to claim the remaining beats. I would never know things like whether or not she preferred sunsets or sunrises, if she'd ever be the kind of person to just get in a car and see how far she could go on a road trip, if she believed in enormous things like heaven and hell, or what dreams she has for her life. But that isn't what it means to know someone. I looked into her eyes as we made love and gave her everything I had, and she showed me every tattered part of her. I know exactly who she is. There was an expectation that I would run away with every new layer she revealed. Only I didn't run away—I ran towards the explosion of delirious, can't possibly last love, as I always do. And I know, that more than anything, she wishes that I had left her in the way that she was used to, so that she could remain unchanged, because that would have been easier.

I get the phone call, and my results are positive. I'm telling Sabrina over text, and I'm telling her that I don't care, but that I just want her to make sure she's taken care of. She doesn't respond, either because she blocked my number, or because she doesn't want to go through the breakup again. All the pieces start to make more sense—that she wasn't apologizing for my bad day, but that she knew. She was actively avoiding me during the entire time she was telling me that she was sick. She thought she had it timed right, and that I wouldn't have gotten it too. But then she became too overwhelmed with guilt, and rather than tell me, she broke up with me, hoping I'd fuck

234

someone on a rebound and blame them. She was afraid—another victim of the fear of intimacy. She couldn't see, she couldn't believe that I wouldn't be angry, she couldn't have known that I would still want her, that I wouldn't look at her with the same disgust she looked at herself. I'm at the clinic, and it's just one pill I have to take—only one pill, to ensure people actually are cured, rather than have extra pills that they willfully skip taking when they feel better. I'm reading the side effects and interactions, when I see that it won't work with anti-depressants. I had been weaning myself off Wellbutrin, but I'm not prepared to give it up outright at this point... I really don't know if I'm going to make it.

In the following days, the rush of memories comes raging back. I'm remembering my history teacher's laugh, big and blustery, how his love for history made me want to be a teacher and my love for history grew from knowing him, and how upsetting it was to be at his funeral. I'm remembering that there were a lot of funerals that year for me. Being the pallbearer at my grandfather's funeral, and how there was a moment where his casket seemed to get lighter— as if his spirit itself was leaving this plane of existence. Looking in on my grandmother near the end as she said, "It's okay, I'm ready." She said it so gently... she was so kind... All these good people are gone, and I'm still here and it's not fair, and sometimes I feel so hurt and alone that I don't know if I can make it. And again I think back to how I was driving then that year, listening to *Yankee Hotel Foxtrot* by Wilco, and I mouthed softly "there is something wrong with me" as I loosened my grip on the steering wheel... Just wanting it all to be over, wanting to crash, and how I lied about it to everyone after I wasn't successful. I'm looking at my forearms, no longer seeing my veins as a beautiful system to transport blood, but instead as maps of where to take a razor blade. I worry about that desire to unlearn the engrained instinct to survive coming back... Like a person being slowly dragged out by the tide, fighting it as long as they can until they succumb to exhaustion. I think about how, in despair, it would be a relief to stop fighting. I'm looking up, always looking up, as I'm falling down.

Grace

How do I forget the contours of your body, my love? How do I dilute and drown your smile, the way you quiver as I make you cum, the salty-sweet taste of your flesh on my tongue? It's like trying to forget the skyline of my childhood, the crisp air and the lightning bugs, it's just there forever. Like rings inside a tree that you can point to, and see its age and changes, so too can you see my loves inside me. I do the only sensible thing, which is to get back on the prowl, back on the grind, keep on hustling. I'm talking to a new girl, Anna Mae, and it very quickly becomes revealed that she's a submissive looking for a master. She's sending me SnapChats regularly of close-up videos of her pussy cumming—a creamy white instead of a clear cum, clear being what I usually prefer. At first, I'm loving our exchanges. She wants me to fuck her mouth "like it's a pussy" and to do anything else I'd like to do. She only exists for me. I'm looking on websites for anal hooks, bondage shackles, Hitachi wand vibrators (with slings to keep them in place), fucking machines, and various restraining devices that I plan to employ on her. Somewhere between looking at these and longing to use them with Sabrina, I realize that the closer I get to someone like Sabrina, the harder it is to move on. After a while she drops off, so I'm looking at porn on my phone, assaulting my senses with debauchery and sounds and moans of other people. I'm not satiated by only messaging girls to say hello and scanning their profiles on OkCupid for common interests to start a conversation. Without the Wellbutrin to fall back on, I have to be faster, messaging even more frequently so that I don't feel alone... I see all the same girls, and ask them outright if they're interested in fucking. One girl I recognize, Brittany, and I remember telling her how pretty she is, and how her eyebrows are immaculate. Good eyebrows, which are vastly under-recognized, usually get a good response when I notice them—they did with Sabrina. A good set of eyebrows are naturally lush, not overly-plucked to be too thin, or ending before the corner of the eye. We have all the same TV shows in common, and all the typical things people say they want in a relationship—only when I messaged her politely before, she never responded. This time, I notice that she's a feminist, and that she says she wants honesty, and that's all she wants in a guy's approach.

So I tell her, "You know what I really want? To please you without necessarily having it returned, only for the pleasure of giving. I want to suck on your massive titties, and lovingly suckle your tiny clit, and shove my tongue deep in your pussy, and finger you until you gush all over my face. And for you to suck on my cock, not because I want you to, but because I want you to want to. Oh, also, your eyebrows are fucking amazing."

"Oh my god I could really go for that.

241

Finally, someone with balls. Here's my number...
And thank you about the eyebrows haha! Text me
;)" I'm texting her, telling her about my hunger for
her. How I'd just lick up and down her pussy and
ass until she screamed in delight, and she texts
back, "Ugh you're perfect". But when I start
throwing in other things I like that we have in
common, she loses interest—it's when I start
becoming a person that she loses interest. She's
spent the better part of a couple of years in
college, defining an ideal partner based not on her
desires but on her politics, and the ideal,
theoretical, submissive agreeable partner will
always be dropped by the wayside for what she
really wants. The flirtation we had is short, and it's
not enough, but really, how much is enough to
bury the memory of a person? How many people
does it take?

I'm talking to a skinny brunette on OkCupid
with a shitty tattoo on her hip that I feign interest
in, and soon enough, she starts talking about sex.

"You know what would be really sexy?"

"If you got down on all fours while I fucked you like an animal?"

"Mmm, exactly that, and if you paid me for sex." I'm remembering on her profile that she's a struggling college kid, and that neither of us know each other's real name.

"Nah, I'm not looking for a prostitute tonight."

"So I take that as a no then?" I don't respond, the emphasis on tonight was lost on her. This becomes a common conversation that I flirt with. I strike up a conversation with a gorgeous, perfectly complexioned, blonde, surfer-girl type. She looks like she could be a model—or maybe she was a model, but got into drugs. She's in Washington D.C., and I think about taking that trip to Baltimore to see my cousin, stopping by the Capitol to see the blonde as well. Her profile says that she's only looking for sugar daddies.

"So, I have a couple questions for you."

"Okay go ahead."

"So like, what are your sexual tastes?"

"I don't have to answer that, so don't judge me for something you know nothing about."

"Oh no, no. I just mean like, can I tell you what I'm into and see if you're into it too?" For some reason, this is perceived as more dignified.

"Sure."

"So, if I were to come to you and just give you a really long massage that ended with fingering you really roughly and fast, would you be okay with that?"

"Sounds nice, actually."

"Okay, well I mean like pretty hard, so that you squirt, and stick my tongue deep in your asshole while I did it, too. What would you want a sugar daddy to do for that?"

"Hm, I think two $100 Amazon gift cards

would be enough for all that." It's true—you really can get anything on Amazon.

Blackmail

I'm messaging an eighteen year old girl on
Plenty of Fish, and she's quickly asking me for my
phone number, leading me to believe that she's
down for a hookup. She's moving to Pennsylvania
from South Carolina in a few months, and I
mention that I'm from Georgia as common ground.
I'm texting her and asking her what her dreams are.
She's telling me that she'd like to have a home, that
she can take care of, and to be able to cook and
clean. Within a few texts, she's asking me to send
her pictures of me, and I oblige with a picture of
me flexing my bicep, and ask for a picture in return.
She's starting to turn sexual in her texts, without a
subtle transition, and I'm bored by the lack of
challenge. I'm responding with all the things I think
she wants to hear: That I'll take her from behind
and grab her hair as I thrust, that I'll choke her as
she cums, that I expect her to swallow. I'm really
only going through the motions, but she loves it all.
She asks for more pictures, and I deny her, telling

her that I'm too tired to take new ones.

"Well when I come up, are we going to have birthday sex?"

I'm now starting to worry that she's not as old as she says and I'm asking her "Well, how old are you going to be?"

"18."

"Well so long as you know we aren't going to do anything in between now and then, if you're okay waiting." It's the next day and I'm at work, starting to get backed up on orders, and my phone is ringing.

"Hello is this Mr. Houston? Sean Houston?"

"Yeah, who's this?"

"I'm the one you have to tell why you're talking to my daughter, and you've got about two minutes to."

"Ohh, oh no. She was on a dating site and she said she was eighteen, and I told her nothing would happen until she was old enough."

"What's wrong with you? I mean, I've read the messages—this is graphic stuff on here. I have a rightful mind to report you to the cops."

"I understand, sir, really, I do. I'm sorry, you know, I was just recently broken up with by my girlfriend, and things just haven't been going my way lately. I understand if that's the way you want to go with things, and you have every right." I have no defense, and I don't want to fake my way through one.

"Well now look, I've already talked to my daughter, and got her to understand that she's not going to see you whatsoever. Her response to that was to punch holes in the wall and busted my damn door down. I've already accepted that, but the thing you really got to worry about is my wife. When she gets home, she's going to throw a fucking fit when she sees this. The only way I can see this being resolved is for this to be taken care of and fixed today."

"I'm sorry to hear that." I'm now talking to him in the bathroom at work, crying and thinking that my life is over.

"Sorry doesn't fix my door."

"Well if there's anything I can do to help out, let me know."

"I'm not concerned about that, trust me, it'll be taken care of. I'm just wanting to know who you are, to know if you're on some sort of list or something. And I'm going to run your name online, and if anything at all comes up about you, I'm going to the police with it."

"I understand, but you won't find anything on me." I'm shaking, literally shaking from anxiety at work, and starting to hyperventilate like when I was a boy. When my phone rings again I jump at the sound.

"Help me to understand what's going

through your mind, and why you talked with her."

"I just, I'm so alone. My girlfriend just broke up with me, and I've taken it very hard. I've been suicidal... I don't really know why I'm telling you this, but I have been in a terrible place."

"All right, well, I looked into you and I didn't see anything. I'm still thinking my wife is going to be a problem, and I think the only way that this is all going to go away is if I get $1,200 dollars today, whatever way you got to get it together to get this door fixed by the end of the day. If it doesn't happen, I know your name and address, and I'll go through all the people you know on Facebook and let them all know what kind of person you are. They're all going to know." They're all going to know—they'll all see the crumbling foundation and tattered spirit of a broken and lonely person. "And I don't want to do this, but I'll go on TV, and I'm sure they'd like nothing more than a story on some predator. I'll go on Good Morning America and destroy you."

"No please, I'll... see what I can do... I'm at work and I can't make it to the bank today. I have to see if I can borrow from a friend." I'm on the phone, barely able to breathe, barely able to speak to a friend to ask to borrow any amount of money.

"Wait, what's the situation again?" He says.

"I was talking to a girl, and it turns out that she wasn't eighteen, and her dad is blackmailing me."

"I don't know man, it just sounds like a scam."

"Please, I can't risk it... I'm really fucking scared, and I just want it to go away."

"Hang on here, I'm actually on my computer looking stuff up and there's actually a story here about a scam on POF where a Southern guy from South Carolina claims his daughter is underage and tries to get hush money, anywhere from $800 to $3,000. Like it sounds way too similar to what you're describing."

"I understand what you're saying... I just, I need the money."

"I think if you do that, there's no way to know that he won't just ask for more money or say those things any way. Honestly dude, it's a scam. I think he just preys on emotionally unstable people, and I don't mean that as an insult, I just know you've been having a hard time. How much do you think it has to do with the breakup?" It has everything to do with it. I go home early, unable to deal with everything there. I'm getting more calls from the supposed father, and I'm telling him that I'm wiring him the money tonight. I turn down his calls, and he sends me a text.

"You want to play games, Mr. Houston? We'll play games." I block him on my phone. I'm sobbing terribly and I see no way out of this, and I'm praying, the sort of unconscious prayer every person prays when everything else has turned to shit—a soft prayer of hope.

Back In The Saddle

I start talking to a girl, Brandy, on OkCupid. She's thin, and is pretty good looking, except that she has a bigger forehead, and her hair doesn't look as naturally soft and straight. She makes it a point in her profile that she's not looking for a one-night stand. "I couldn't agree more on how silly hookups are. I mean, don't get me wrong, I love sex and everything."

"Yeah, I mean I love sucking dick, I just want someone to love, too." She's asking me for pictures of my abs, my second least favorite set of muscles, and she's disappointed that I'm so hairy. After receiving my picture she says, "there's something I need to tell you."

"Okay..."

"Listen, this is so stupid, and not a big deal, but I was born a guy." Brandy or Brandon?

"Oh, so, like, you had the surgery?"

"No, not yet, I still have a pickle in my pants haha. But I don't want anything done for me anyway. I really love pleasing and having sex and taking it in my ass, plus I'm on hormones."

"Are you like, going to get the surgery?"

"Eventually, why?" I'm thinking about all the girls I've kissed, how every part of them was feminine, and I think of the over 2,500 differences in genes between us. How their lips were extensions of their strands of DNA, how their breasts would slope down their body, how they have beautiful hips for my hands to rest on and tight wet pussies that reacted to my touch. I can't wrap my mind around wanting to pursue someone who could only ever technically be a female through science and a vivid imagination to me. She's sweet, and she's been fucked over by too many guys who didn't come to grips with their bisexuality for me to lead her on into thinking that I could want her in that way. But I still view her as a person, as worthy as anyone else of love and I want

254

her to be able to find happiness, so I let her down gently, and tell her that I'm sure there's someone for her.

It's the first day I'm talking to another girl online, and I'm telling her about how I, too, like flipping through Netflix—the new opioid of the masses. "I would also give you massages while you watched Netflix haha :3"

"Are you good at massages?"

"You would be out of your mind, and I adore giving them. My hands are so strong, but gentle when needed. I can go for a while too, and if you have lotion it's even better ;)"

"Well, Sean, I'm not about to complain at the thought of you giving me a massage ;)"

"And I'd rub down your back, all the way down your adorable thighs while kissing and licking your neck."

"And then..."

"I'd take my hand, and start rubbing up and down your pussy, making you ache with desire."

"Baby I'm getting so wet... Tell me more."

"Well, the reason I'm so good at massage, aside from my strong hands, is that I love doing it. I love making a girl feel good, and because of that, I'm amazing at it. And that love of giving and pleasing translates into other things... I would tenderly encircle your little nipples, until they were hard and overly sensitive to the touch. But I wouldn't stop there—I would lightly trace them all the way down to your clit, and with just two fingers gently stroke up and down while I was kissing you. And with just two fingers, I could make you cum in seconds. But with all of those orgasms you'd start to have, I'd have to start licking your pussy, and in between licking, go back to kiss you so that you tasted yourself on my lips." She's asking if my cock is hard for her, and saying how badly she wants to suck on it, but it's only because she's so horny. When she finally climaxes over the sexy messages,

256

she blocks me on the site, ashamed of so easily releasing herself to the passion.

I'm texting a girl who makes out with her sister for Tumblr, except her texts are only coming through as squares. I screenshot my phone to show her, and when she realizes my phone is out of date and isn't accepting her emojis, I never hear from her again. There's another woman I see on OkCupid in an open relationship, but I don't want any part of that swan song. I'm reading a message on OkCupid from a twenty year old girl who's saying that she's looking to get off the site, and she gives me her SnapChat instead. She has big, perky breasts, and supple red lips that could make me do anything. She's snapping me pics and asks me to send her some of me. I flex and take a picture of my bicep while smirking casually, and take another with my shirt off. She responds with a topless picture, and her breasts look as perky without a bra. Her almost brownish nipples make me wonder if she's Jewish. "I want to see your ass" I'm telling her, and she complies, and somehow takes a picture of her on all fours, ass high in the air. I'm visiting her the next day at Karn's grocery store, where she works, because she mentioned that she wanted to meet. "Why hello there," I'm saying with a big smile on my face, and she shyly looks away, embarrassed that she's blushing, but I'm playing it off as though I don't notice.

"Hi... You're so tall..." She says softly, while tucking her hair behind her ear, exposing her neck to me.

"Yeah, I suppose that means you'll have to stand on your tip toes to give me kisses." I start laughing, and she's blushing more. "Well look, I don't want to get you in trouble or anything from talking too long." I'm turning my head, looking around for a manager, and also showing off how my traps and shoulders look in my tight shirt.

"No, that's okay, I doubt I'll get in trouble." She's relaxed now, looking down at my crotch, but trying to look away when I make eye contact with her. I find a lull in the conversation, and tell her that I'll talk to her later, to leave her wanting more. "You're really cute, like really really cute ;)" She texts after I leave.

"Yeah? What did you like about me? Haha indulge me ;)"

"Well I liked your arms, they're fucking huge. And I like your butt, I kept on picturing things..."

"What, like grabbing it?"

"Yeah..."

"I thought I saw you looking at my crotch :P"

"Oh my gosh... Yeah... I totally was."

"And what were you thinking of?"

"I was thinking about sucking your cock, if I'm being honest."

"Oh, I think I like the sound of that :)" A few

hours go by, and she is using the messenger on SnapChat to tell me that she needs to tell me something. There's no way she can be a guy with those tits, I'm thinking, shaking my head, when she tells me that she's with someone. "Oh..."

"I just, I love him, and I just can't keep talking to you. I'm also 16." I'm hit with the atom bomb, grateful that she doesn't want to talk anymore. After a few minutes, she texts me, "Promise me you'll remember me?"

"Yeah, of course."

I'm flipping between Tinder and OkCupid again. There's a girl in Selinsgrove that I would consider meeting, as she's only about an hour away from Harrisburg. I'm looking through her sex related questions on the site. She likes being called a good girl—she says it's her weakness. She likes anal and giving head, and everything else is a cherry on top. "You seem like such a good girl :) I definitely like girls that are a touch awkward at first

;)"

"Someone paid attention to the questions
:p"

"Oh I definitely did, I'm taking great
pleasure in reading them. :) Are you taking
pleasure in reading mine? I hope I made it very
clear that I have a love of foreplay :)"

"Oh yes, I've noticed. I'm a big fan of
foreplay, too, it's just not as good if I'm not worked
up first!"

"To me, foreplay is everything. I could
spend eternities licking and suckling your nipples,
all for your delight."

"That's really hot, like every part of that
message. I'm also somewhat delirious and not
usually this blunt about sex... But here we are!"

"I have a disarming quality as well, so it's
not entirely your fault ;) I like being blunt, no
bullshit, you know? I'm also very confrontational,

direct, and commanding. I send food back if it's made wrong, instead of meekly eating something I don't enjoy. And planets would collide as I sucked and licked your clit as well. For the sake of being blunt, I hunger for your pleasure :)"

"Commanding sounds like it would be perfect for me in bed. I am very submissive. I mean, I can take control if I'm told to, but for the sake of being blunt, in the bedroom I just want to be someone's little slut. In an endearing way." I believe I'm one of the few people who knows exactly how endearing she means. "And hot damn... I'm sure you'd be seeing the same stars when I take you deep in my throat. Fun secret? I love giving head... I swear I'm not usually all about sex. It's just one of those nights."

"Of course in an endearing way, all I've ever wanted is a cum-hungry slut that lived to serve me. It's so hot. I usually get too into giving of pleasure to receive, but I very much so want to tell you, with my hard cock in front of your face 'open your mouth.' And without question, of course, you would, and I'd slide in and out of your mouth, and you would take it all gratefully."

"That. Is so. Hot. You have no idea how much I love reading messages like this. I'm getting super worked up." I'm picking out my outfit to drive to see her tonight. I know she's in the palm of my hand, and already soaking through her panties.

"You should know that I'm a hopeless romantic deep down. So when I tell you to get on all fours, and to arch your ass up high; for my tongue to go as deep as possible in your ass, that the pleasure is out of affection. And as I'm tongue-ing your asshole, I'll tell you to rub your clit for me, while I start to finger you deeply. But not fast, or hard, just caressing your G-spot, feeling it starting to get hard from my touch. Your orgasm building..."

"Oh my god, that's like... that's like,

perfect."

"If you surrendered your pussy to my rough and fast fingering, I could easily make you gush. You and I would be covered in your pussy juices, and I would get more carnal and turned on... And you would have a string of the most intense orgasms you'll ever know..."

"My pussy is throbbing... I have squirted before, you know. Not often, but it's possible."

"What if I told you I could make you squirt in actual seconds? Does that make your pussy throb even more?"

"I'll surrender to you any day ;) OMG yes, yes yes yes... How do you not have a girlfriend, holy shit."

"I'm clingy and I can't pretend to not be interested..." I realize I'm starting to reveal something deeper to her, and I'm going back to the sexual talk for fear of being rejected based on who I am. "I want you to be on all fours for me, a slave to my sexual whims, and to reach back and take my cock in your hands and slowly slide it into your ass. I not only want to do that with you, but I want you to want it. And I want for you to want to taste yourself on my cock, with each thrust into you for you to think about me pulling out of you, shoving my aching cock in your mouth, and you savoring every second of it as you look up into my eyes. Make me ache, start moaning as you suck my head, milking the cum out. You'll hunger for it like a good girl."

"I mean, I know we're obviously into sex, but I would be down to get to know you too," she messages me as I'm typing my longer message. "Holy fuck, oh my goddd, I want to be your good girl. I just want you to bend me over in my bed right now and fuck me. Fuck me and then turn me around and fuck me more and choke me while I moan and cum all over your cock. And then choke me again but this time with your fucking cock in my throat. I wanna lick up all my juices dripping from your cock holy hell... I bet you'd pin me down to the bed before we're even undressed..."

"Have you ever desired someone as you have with me?" I think back to Sabrina, and her dutiful nature, and wonder where she is right now.

"Never, omg, I want you so bad right now... Secret: I'm touching myself and I never masturbate, ever."

"I'm sure you're rubbing your clit, but I want you to stick a finger inside yourself for me. And to picture my much thicker, longer fingers, and later my cock inside you instead while I kiss you and our tongues massage each other."

"It feels so good, oh my god, I don't usually like to fuck myself, but I'm just so worked up I have to."

"I want you to tell me, that I can fuck you whenever I want to. Like, if I'm free Thursday, or tonight, and I want to come over and yank your panties down, that I can. Surrender yourself... And

266

keep fingering yourself, and pull your finger out with your pussy juices on it and suck them off. Describe your taste to me."

"Fuck me, omg, fuck me hard any fucking day... It was juicy and sweet and kinda sticky... come taste it yourself baby."

"And what if I just want to come over to rim your asshole, nothing more than to just build you up to an impossible level of horniness? Tell me I can do that too."

"Yes baby, yes, anything you want, oh my god I'm so wet. I'll lick you up and down, all over your balls and your cock, I'll get you hard any time you're around me... But you won't be able to resist squeezing your hard cock inside my tight pussy any time you're near me."

"Is that to say that you'll always want me to fuck you?"

"Always." The promise is only in the heat of the moment. The next day, there are no new messages, and I'm asking her if she's busy or if she just feels guilty about sexting so early on, when she doesn't respond to my previous message. "Is both an option?" She showed me everything about herself, without showing me anything at all. I'm finding myself looking up Sabrina's Facebook, something we'd never exchanged. In her profile picture, she's with a younger guy, acne-riddled face, and they're both smirking. It's obvious she has something that in all my prowess to give her endless orgasms I couldn't give her—happiness. I'm relieved, and in a way I'm overjoyed that I know she's okay.

Maddie

I'm messaging a dirty blonde, Maddie, on POF, and she's nineteen, soon to be twenty. I quickly receive a message back, and she's asking me if I can give her money for a lap dance.

"Well I do think you're really cute, but what's this money for?" I'm asking her, hoping that I can see her without it.

"My dad died last year, and I need the money to support my mom and brothers. I was stripping before, but I got fired from the job over a misunderstanding about my schedule. Do you think you can meet me tonight?"

"Well... I've been burned before, so how do I know you aren't a catfish?" Or worse... She gives me her SnapChat, and snaps pictures of herself and I'm put at ease. "Well look, do you think... you could see being into me without the money? I mean like, I'd love to take care of you and help you out for a little bit, but after all that is over, I'd like to be your boyfriend for real."

"Yeah, that'd be amazing. I mean you're like my hero, pretty much. I was needing $200, because that's what the electric company needs before the power is shut off."

"I only have $60 extra dollars, but I don't want a lap dance... I just want to help you." Because I can't help myself...

"Anything will help. I'll see about getting my brothers out of the house." I'm at the address she gave me, and I'm greeted by an older woman, who is telling me a Maddie doesn't live there. I'm thinking that I knew it was too good to be true, I'm about to leave when I see she snapped me that she's actually next door, that she was worried I wouldn't show. I'm led to her place, and I'm sitting on her couch, which is covered in cat hair. I take my hat off, and we start kissing. She's a shy, timid kisser, and as she subtly pulls away, I wonder what's in her, deep down.

She's leading me up the steps, to her mom's bedroom. We're laying down and she's taking her top off. I'm kissing her soft nipples, and she's looking at me wide-eyed. "I just want to take care of you, to help you. I don't want you doing those things with other guys."

"I won't. It'll be hard, but it's better for me this way." I'm accepting that this is what I've come to, paying for love because I can't afford to be alone, at least for a little while. "My brothers will be back soon, and I'm going to my grandma's house this weekend. She doesn't have Wi-Fi there, so I won't be able to talk after tonight." I give her the $60, and I'm hugging her, and telling her I know it will get better for her. I have to believe that it will for her, so that it will for me.

The following Thursday, I'm at her house again, after just cashing my paycheck, and I'm planning to give her $150 more dollars. I'm hoping that this is enough... That her electric bill will be paid, and that we can start something real, to have a chance again in life, for this amount to somehow be enough to rescue me from depression. Maybe there's a part of myself in her I can still rescue. Her mom, who Maddie told about our arrangement, comes outside with a big smile on her face. "It's so nice to meet you, Sean. I hope to see a lot more of you." She seems perfectly content to be her madam, and it's becoming more evident how wrong this situation is, but I can't help myself. I just want to make her happy in the ways I was unable to with other girls. Her mom takes off with her brothers, and we're upstairs in her room again.

"I want to make it so that you're getting something out of this... I want to give you a blowjob, but I also want it to be like we talked about. I want it to be real, and I want it to happen whenever it's supposed to happen."

"I do, too," I'm saying, while grabbing her ass, "and before anything happens, I want you to feel safe and secure." I'm telling myself that I can't give her any more money this week, that the

272

remaining $200 I have in my checking account is for bills I have to pay next week. Only when it comes, and she's asking me for more, I'm driving to the grocery store, desperately trying to use the cash back option for debit purchases, but I can't remember my password... I try my bank, and they happen to be open late. I'm again upstairs in her house, money in my pocket, and she's horny. She's telling me about how good I've been to her, and I'm getting hard at the praise. She slips off into the bathroom for a minute, and when she comes out, she shyly pulls down her pants. I've been dreaming of that wonderful pink tumescence of life ever since I laid eyes on her. It's felt like a lifetime since I last ate pussy, and I can't control my urges any longer. She's laying back, her legs spread for me, and it's ever so plump—I can see that blood has been flowing through her all day waiting for this moment too. She has a barely visible clit, it's so tiny, and I'm sucking on the entirety of it and her pussy. Something is off... it's tasteless, and odorless, and I'm realizing she likely douched herself in the bathroom, which is disappointing. I'm happily tonguing away, but she's not enjoying it like I want her to, and my hard on fades. Who am I if I can't please? The door downstairs opens, and it's her mom. I have to sneak out quietly. Before I go, I'm giving her the money, looking at her pupils dilating, and I'm telling her, "This is it. This is all the money I have. If we're going to make it, if we're going to be anything, it has to be more than this, okay?"

She's shaking her head yes, and I'm driving away, hopeful that it will get better. It's only a few days before she's telling me again about another bill, and I know as I've always known that it's not a real bill. I'm telling her that I'm flat broke, that I haven't had money for groceries. "I should've never stopped giving people lap dances. They gave me way more money than you ever did anyway."

274

Daddy's Little Girl

I've sent a few messages to an eighteen year old waifish brunette, that calls herself Kitty, who claims to be asexual, and I'm very polite as I discuss various points on her profile, because I want it to be long term with her. There's some mystique about her, and when she doesn't answer, it makes me stupidly want her more. I wait two weeks before messaging her again, hoping that she deleted my original message. "I love all your pictures, you're so lovely and I keep picturing kissing your creamy ivory thighs."

"Wow, thank you very much :) I'm sure my thighs would highly appreciate it lol," she replies within a few minutes.

"Oh really now? I should warn you, I wouldn't know when to stop kissing them all over ;) I love giving massages too, my hands are meant to be caressing :)"

"God, that's hot!!! You really got me going

tonight ughhh :p I'm Carly btw"

"Hi Carly, would you also like to hear about my tongue? When I would kiss your thighs, I would also be using my tongue, leaving little wet kisses all over. Would you like that?"

"You make me such a naughty virgin, mmm you make my pussy feel so good just by dirty talking with me... fuuuck." I'm looking at her pictures, already achingly hard, and I'm unsure if she's actually a virgin, but I like the thought of it.

"Mmhmm, I bet you taste so sweet, would you like my tongue tasting your cute little pussy? Inside you deeply licking, and taking it out to swirl over your clit?"

"God I need you to tongue fuck me... I want you to bite my thigh and shove a finger right into my tiny hole... It would hurt so much, but mmmm, I need your fingers in me..." She's touching herself, getting off on releasing herself to her buried sexual side.

276

"I'll come over right now, not even for sex or anything for me, just to give you as many orgasms as your tiny pussy can handle. My big, strong fingers man handling you. Well when you surrender your pussy to me, that is :)"

"I want to be your fucking slave... Your cock warmer... Be my daddy and own this pussy. I can just imagine me on your bed... you throwing me down, holding me down, and just insanely fucking me... Mmm daddy please pop my cherry I can't handle it." I'm thinking of collars, ropes, and completely dominating her until she's dizzy with lust, but I'm asking her a question to see if she's ready.

"What is your sole purpose as my little girl and slave?"

"To serve you whenever and wherever you want or need... Your cock would be the only thing I think about... the only thing I want... I want your cum inside my stomach every day, every hour..."

I've never fully embraced the role of a "daddy" in the sense of a little girl daddy-type relationship, and I'm looking up information on Google, and it seems close enough to a master-type relationship that I'm rolling with it, even though I feel a little silly using the language.

"Your daddy wants to fuck you, whenever he wants it." Still living to please, I tap into her desire to please, and I'm turned on at the thought of her being turned on by being used, and aching as badly as I do to please. "And I want you to think about it every day, each passing moment just aching for my touch again. And you need to drink your master's cum to survive, don't you?"

"God yes... I need your fingers, your mouth, your cum... But I need your amazing cock filling me up right now... Mmm it hurts so bad daddy, soo bad... I can't even breathe, I need you. My body is yours, clean and pure... I want you to defile me, make me your slutty baby girl daddy."

"Is your tight pussy only going to be satisfied by your masters hard cock? Thrusting up into you, each thrust more powerful than the last, your master's hands around your neck choking you a little as you moan and whimper?" I'm trying to switch from daddy to master, for the sake of ease in sexting. "And when I'm going to cum, I expect you on all fours sucking it out of me. Grateful for me fucking your mouth, thanking me for cumming in your mouth, and begging for more."

"Oh my god... I'm so close, take whatever you want, whatever you need. Wrap your big hand around my tiny neck and, mm, shove your thick cock right where it belongs... In my daddy's hole... I want to cum on your cock... Mhmmm and your warm cum going right into my tummy." I'm not going to win the daddy/master word tug of war, so I just go with it.

"I have a leash and collar for you, light pink and cute. You'll wear it, and love that I'm pulling on it as I'm fucking you from behind. Tell me that you'll love it, that you'll love being your daddy's fuck slut."

"Daddy, I just need you... Nothing else matters. Every day I will live to satisfy you, your living little sex doll. Mmm, you seriously make my whole pussy ACHE for you. We haven't even met, and my little pussy just needs you... Daddy, I love being your fuck slut, your little whore who lives to be on your huge cock. Daddy, you need to fill my aching pussy, it hurts so bad... Your fingers, cock, tongue... And I would wear your collar everyday... to show who's my owner, that no one can ever satisfy me like my daddy."

"Be my slave, and my little girl. Your daddy will keep you safe, and give you all the pleasure you can handle. Your master will tell you what to do, and you will obey. You should just be my girlfriend already. We'll go on cute dates, and then we'll end each day with you cumming endlessly as your daddy fucks you. And if you're a bad little girl and don't do as your daddy commands, you'll be punished :)"

"Mmm, you know that's what I want. You deserve my pussy, it was practically made for you... And I just imagine that I will probably enjoy these punishments no matter what :P" I'm getting in the shower, hoping to see her tonight, knowing full well I will have everything I want. But she doesn't respond to my next couple of messages, so I wait a few days, and it's as though my entire body is on fire with wanting her. A completely innocent-looking girl, giving into the throws of debauchery. Finally, she messages me again. "So sorry I haven't messaged back, I've just been so busy lately. Can you forgive me? :(" It didn't work out with the other person she was talking to, is what she's really saying.

"Tell your daddy something sweet and I'll think about it :)"

"How about I tell you how the last time we talked, you made me cum so hard in my panties... I got in the shower and cleaned my little pussy thinking all about daddy. These past few days, I just couldn't stop thinking about you, and how you made me feel so good with just your words. I've never wanted an older man more than I want you... No one interests or pleases me more than my daddy and I miss you so much :("

"Daddy forgives you. You are all I want. I ache for you. I just wish I was licking your sweet pussy right now. You need to be my little girl :)"

"I am your little girl, I need you... My body needs you, I can't even explain it. I just need you to touch me, anywhere, do anything to me... God, you would fuck me so good, I just want to cum thinking about it. You would treat my little body so right with your big hands and tongue."

"What would you say if I told you that I could make you cum in literal seconds? Just one, quick, hard, fast sliding in of two of my thick fingers, barely fitting in your tight pussy, massaging your G-spot until your pussy started making a puddle beneath you. I can finger for an hour on end, until my forearms are too filled with blood to move, and then I just will tongue and lick until there's nothing left in either of us. This is your gift from me: Take it all :)"

"Daddy, you are so good to me. I want to cry because of how amazing you are to me. My little hole clenches up even at the mention of your fingers. I need you to fill me up, Daddy." She makes a point of capitalizing Daddy—that's my name to her. "I need your fingers deep in my virgin pussy and your warm tongue on my clitty :) Suck me and bite me, Daddy... Drink me all up. Then I need you to grab my wrists and hold me down... Suck on my little pink tongue and make me taste my own pussy juice... You're my perfect man, my god, and my master. I just know my little pussy was made to be yours, yours to use. When we're together, I don't think I will be able to last even a minute without your cock inside one of my holes...

I need you to touch my body so badly, from my hairless little pussy to my little titties made for your hands and mouth :) I want you to be constantly pressed inside me, my body warming your yummy cock. The thought of your cum literally makes me drool, licking and suckling your precious cum out of the head of your cock..." You are the yin to my yang, my equal in depravity.

"Clearly, you need to be my girlfriend. Right now. And I love your titties, and think about torturing you by sucking on your nipples until they hurt the next day. I want them to brush against your bra, or your shirt if you're bra-less, and for you to ache and think of me. I want even just the thought of my fingers tracing around your nipples to leave a puddle in your panties. I want there to be a need for you to have spare panties on you, from soaking through them so often throughout your adorable day. When I showered after our conversation the other day, pre-cum was oozing out of my cock, and I thought, what a waste: My cute cum slave deserved every drop of it. I want to give you a minimum of two, ideally four, servings each day we're together. Have to keep my little girl healthy :) Being with me would consist of you feeling safe, warmed by my big strong body, you getting fucked and cuddling to *The Office*. What do you think of that, honey? :)"

"Yes Daddy, my little pink nipples are all puffy waiting for you :) Mmm, definitely at least four feedings from Master's cock a day. Suckling and swallowing all of your cum down to my tummy. I think that would be perfect, Daddy, just you petting and cuddling with me would be perfect, and make me feel so warm and safe :) I need your big body pressing against my little one at all times, holding on to your little girl. I think I could easily fall in love with my daddy and his perfect body that takes care of me. My body just cannot stop aching for you. I would do anything for you, even eat your cum all day long. Honestly, your cum is the only thing I want to keep me full. Just imagine me on my knees in front of you, suckling and deep throating master's cock, and drinking all of your cum down while I looked into my Daddy's eyes so satisfied and happy :)) Nothing would make me happier than your hairy and big balls in my mouth, my face nestled in your pubes... There's a piece missing from me, Daddy, and you need to fill it." I'm falling faster and faster for what can only turn into co-dependency, and I don't care because I'm delirious with desire.

"How did you know they were hairy? Now your pussy on the other hand, daddy wants to be hairless. I would do my very best to keep your adorable tummy full of my cum, I'm sure I can make enough for you to have a serving every hour. Of course, it'll always be available to you, warm and fresh from the tap ;) I expect you to not break eye contact with your Daddy as I cum in your mouth, and to look at me so thankful and happy. You're so perfect, and I want to be yours and only yours, always :)"

"Just a good guess, and I would love a hairy daddy rubbing against my smooth, hairless body. And of course, Daddy, my sweet baby pussy would always be nice and shaved and pink for you :) Daddy, lock me up in your house to make sure that I'm always yours... Oh Daddy, I can just imagine you fucking me over the kitchen counter or holding me nice and tight on your lap with your cock deep inside me while you eat your breakfast. Or how about me under the table giving you a nice, long blowjob, sucking down all of Daddy's essence. Even if Daddy has to go pee, his baby will drink it all up for him and continue warming his big cock in my little mouth :)" When I think that maybe I misread her text, she sends me another message "Piss down my throat, Daddy :)" I have no moral outrage, I don't turn down her offer to debase her—in fact I'm embracing it because I want to see how far down I can go. The agony and the ecstasy of lust for the sake of lust.

She sends me a picture of her panties

around her knees, her fingers stretching sticky wetness from them, and I'm telling her that I need to see her tonight. She's unsure, as she's staying in Gettysburg with her parents, but she agrees she wants to see me tonight. I'm freshly showered, and I'm on my way to Gettysburg without an address or a definite answer from her—just heading in the direction of Gettysburg. I'm completely possessed by her, and I'm salivating and not able to even focus on the road. An almost ravenous want comes over me. I'm driving around aimlessly, circling around the general area of Gettysburg waiting for her to text me back. I'm drunk on the idea of someone wanting me again, and I'm desperately hoping that feeling will last. I've been sitting at a gas station for the last hour waiting for a response that never comes, and the door to these new kinks closes. I think more about her, wanting to find her somehow in the world to pin her down and own her for the rest of her life.

288

Baptism

I'm on my way to a girl's house, Leah, and I
have a small window before her mom or sister get
home. We talked about me using her dildos on
her, and fucking her pussy and ass at the same time
with them, and how I would make her gush with
my hands, but if there wasn't any chemistry, we'd
watch Gilmore Girls. "Netflix and Gil?" I ask her,
and when I have to explain the joke after she
doesn't get it the first time, she replies with "LOL".
I want to fuck her mercilessly, for some reason, and
I want it to go further than we talked about. The
TV is playing in the background when I walk in, and
we're sitting there semi-awkwardly watching it.
She's nervous, and she's making up her mind
whether she wants me or not. We move to her
bedroom, I'm rubbing her shoulders and undoing
her bra. She has F-cup breasts, but her nipples are
smaller and more like a B-cup's. I'm hungrily
sucking on them, rubbing her razor bumped pussy
as I do. I'm fingering her, and she starts squirting

as I'm getting hard. The urge to take my pants off and start pounding her is building. Then she starts to have these crying type whimper orgasms, like a Japanese porn star, and I find it strange and start getting soft. We start watching Gilmore Girls for a few minutes, and she off-handedly complains about the wet spot I made. Her cat is coming into the bedroom, and she's starting to pet him. I'm asking for a cup of water, and as I'm drinking it, we're both having the same thought of me leaving, which I do.

There's a cute college girl named Kay, who is really short at barely 5 feet tall, and I'm kissing her on the York campus' grass under the stars. I'm putting my hand down her pants and she's already cumming after just a few seconds. Her G-spot was tucked up inside her a little deeper, but I could still touch it and feel it getting hard, and right as she's orgasming again, someone walks by with their dog. She plays it off cool, but puts a stop to going any further. When I get home, I'm doing grip exercises, not satisfied with how difficult it was to get her off. While I'm squeezing my plate-loaded gripper, I'm seeing on the shelf in the closet a teddy bear that I bought for my nephew. I never gave it to him, because I was too scared that he wouldn't like it. It pops into my head that it's his baptism in the morning, and I head over to my parents' house, where I sleep on the couch so that they can wake me up so I don't miss it.

There's a bunch of jostling around, it seems like it's morning, and my nephew is running around and laughing only the way a child can. I hear my mom whisper, "Be quiet, we don't want to wake Uncle Sean."

"I'm already up, when's the baptism?"

"Well, we already went to it."

"Mom, I took off work to make sure I would be able to go, and it's why I came here last night," I'm saying, groggy and irritable. I wanted to start over too... to be new.

"Well, you looked like you could've used the sleep, Sean. I'm sorry."

"I just have had a hard week of working and hitting the gym pretty hard. I wish I could work a little less."

"Well what do you want to do with your life?" She asks me, the same question she always asks when I'm there, while making coffee. How do I tell her I'm a fucked up artist with not enough talent or direction?

"I just want someone to love." I say softly, too softly for her to hear.

A Desire To Be In Grace

I'm in Wal-Mart buying new dress shirts and ties to get ready for my first week of a new job, and I wonder if maybe a higher paying job will lead to a relationship. I almost drop my phone while looking through OkCupid, because I see that a girl, Grace, I talked to a few years ago is back on again. She had left Pennsylvania to live with her sister in Boston. She is a twenty-six year old full-time model, who has the problem of scaring away guys because of how attractive she is. I'm relating to a lot of what she's saying, about looking for someone she could see herself being with long term—maybe not settle down right away, but someone more serious. It's non-committal enough to wiggle out of a new relationship if need be. But I've already pushed in all my chips, and my brain is hit with a clusterfuck of neurons over-firing serotonin and dopamine. We're texting daily about little things, and I'm playing it conservatively, trying to be cool. There's a strange and new absence of wanting to rush to a date, but I'm telling her that this upcoming Friday I'm taking her out to a nice restaurant, and she likes that I'm telling her it's going to happen.

After several catfish experiences, I am at least entertaining the idea that her images were just stolen, and aren't who she really is, so that I at least won't let out an uncontrolled gasp like the last few times that has happened to me. I'm wearing one of the newer dress shirts and a tie I bought, and I'm contemplating a sports jacket. I'm wanting to send the message that I'm not trying too hard, though, so I skip the jacket. I freshly shave my head and face, leaving my goatee and mustache. I have a reservation for Accomac, a higher-end restaurant in York by a little river, and I leave myself an extra half hour to make sure that I'm on time. I'm almost always either right on time or late, and I'm wanting to make a good first impression with her. I'm sitting in my car at Accomac, looking out at the river while making sure my tie is tight. When she arrives, time slows down like we're in a movie because she's so damned beautiful. My heart is pounding. Her hair is perfectly side parted, but the wind is flowing softly through it, as if to say that she's connected to everything. She's smiling at me, saying that she's glad I'm really who I said I was, and we both are telling each other catfish stories as we walk to the restaurant. I'm walking behind her, looking at her ass in her dress as she walks, and my hand could easily cup the majority of her ass cheek she's so petite.

"We're going to have the charcuterie board—that just sounds too adorable not to order. And I'll have a water, and a coffee." I'm ordering very directly, catching from the corner of my peripheral vision that her eyes are fixated on my lips, and her pupils are dilating. She is the feminine ideal—people will undergo surgeries, endless hours in the gym, and dieting to not even come close to her genetic perfection—and I want to match her by being the masculine ideal. After placing our order,

I'm looking at her eyes and they're watery. She sneezes, and I'm saying "Bless you, is everything okay? Do you have allergies?" It's her normalcy behind the perfection that I like—the slightly stubbly armpits, the watery eyes, the things she is embarrassed about that I could fall for.

"Yes, I'm sorry. I took a Benadryl before leaving, but it's not working, apparently."

"It's okay, here." I'm handing her my cloth napkin, smiling, and I feel like my face is red with blushing. "Ah so finally, we get to have our date." We both giggle a little. "What was Boston like?"

"It was okay. I was there mostly to be with my sister. And well, I was dating this guy for a while that lived there, but that didn't work out, obviously."

"I'm sure he was just a douche."

"He definitely was," and we both start laughing.

"Ah so where does that put me then, in comparison to all those other hundreds of guys hitting you up?"

She's blushing, not able to maintain eye contact for long. "Very high up."

"Oh yeah?" I'm saying with a grin, "What exactly was it that did it for you?" I start faking a yawn in an obvious way, because I'm flexing my muscles, and she laughs at the gesture.

"Well it was that you actually asked me out—that was a big part of it. And you're like, the most attractive guy I've ever talked to."

"Well I don't understand not wanting to ask you out—I mean, I desire you, and if I want it to lead anywhere with you why wouldn't I? That'd just be a pussy move to not ask you out."

"Pretty much" she says, and we're both laughing, both blushing. "The other thing is, I really like that you don't drink. I was doing a bit too much of it with the modeling, and I'm trying to stick to the full-time job and not drink." Our charcuterie board comes out.

"Oh look how *cute* it is." I say, and she smiles. "I'm glad too. It's hard finding someone whose existence isn't defined by getting trashed all the time," I'm saying, and she's very politely eating little pieces of charcuterie and asking me about my favorite shows. I'm telling her that I like *Breaking Bad*, but I'm being down to earth and relatable at the same time by sheepishly confessing that I love reality TV too.

"Oh, my mom is obsessed with reality TV, and as a result so am I, but she'll like cry over it and it's funny, and a little sad," and she laughs.

"Man, that's fucking adorable." I unconsciously plant a sexual thought in her brain. "I gotta say, I think this is going really well. I think you should come over here and give me a smooch."

"I think you should come over here and kiss

me." Without hesitation, in front of the other customers, I get up and start French kissing her while standing in front of her. I lose track of how long I've been kissing her, when our main dishes are brought out.

"That was nice. Ahh, now we can eat without all that crazy tension." She's blushing, worked up from the kiss, and I'm playing it cool. Later I'm at her car, she's rubbing the backs of my hands as I'm squeezing her breasts hard. She's wild and free, and the urge to tame her overwhelms me. She's taking my tongue in her mouth, but she pulls away so that she turns around for me to grab her ass, and I'm grabbing it in such a way that I'm rubbing her pussy. Everything is so tight and perfect, and my cock is aching rubbing against her. I'm kissing her neck, letting her feel how hard my cock is, as I move my hands back up to her perfect breasts. Two joggers trot by in the distance, and she says while almost gasping from the fondling and kissing that she doesn't want to get caught, and I roar "I don't care" as I continue to caress her. She turns to face me, and my hand is rubbing her pussy lips and clit over her dress, I can feel that it's tiny. There's no friction, and it's likely perfectly waxed and smooth and hairless. She is the first sound of rain on a rooftop, the feeling of freedom you have on an open road, and I want her, deserve her. I'm kissing her breasts—just the cleavage, because I want to leave her wanting more.

"I can be kind of a chore to get off," she's saying, as she's on the cusp of an orgasm.

"That's okay, I like doing chores," I say and smirk.

"I should get home... to feed the cats."

"Well you know, I could go with you. But I'd very much so like to come over tomorrow as well, is that what you want, too?"

"Definitely," she says, looking to her car, almost gesturing for me to get in. I'm pressing her up against her car again, grabbing her ass, manhandling her. I'm fighting the urge to yank down her panties and tongue her endlessly, but I really want it to work out with her—I want to build our intimacy and then be physical, instead of the other way around. We both want a long-term relationship, we both could have random hookups if we really wanted to, and it feels good taking it a little slower.

I drive home, texting her "I really like you :)" before pulling over to the side of the road to start jerking off.

"I really like you too, Sean :)" She replies back, touching herself as well, I'm sure. The next day we have plans for a date, but she texts "I'm so sorry, my allergies are really bad today."

"Aww, that's okay, we'll have plenty of time for dates in the future :)" She doesn't reply. I let a day pass, and text her that I hope she feels better. A few more days pass, and I'm texting her again, and then I crack and start telling her too much about myself, and about my wretched and pathetic history of failures. It doesn't matter—I've been blocked and ghosted, no explanation was simply easier for her. The non-communication is her answer, I just can't accept it yet. Whoever cares less has all the power. I'm stalking her Facebook, seeing her doing more modeling, having left the full-time job she so positively talked about. I can't criticize her too harshly, because something breaks inside me at the new job, and I too go back to what I know. It looks like she started drinking again as well, and while I'm thumbing through pictures, I see that a girl comments on one of her pictures that she misses her, and she wants to know how she's doing.

"I'm doing all right, I can't seem to find a guy that's interesting for more than a few hours though lol." I block her Facebook page. I don't want to search for her anymore, and I want to feel as though I'm ending things on my terms, even though it's long been over. I was the embodiment

302

of getting old to her, a safety, a backup plan for when she finally wants to give up partying. I'm driving aimlessly around, cursing that it just doesn't want to fucking work out for me... So, I'm on Tinder again. I keep on drinking the poison that is pleasure, expecting the antidote to somehow be at the bottom of the bottle...

I find a cute girl who's into massages and snuggling, "yeah cuddling is really underrated," I say, disinterestedly. She's a little tipsy when she comes into my place. She's laying on top of me on my couch, and it's sinking in a little because it's starting to show its age. She laughs as she falls in a little bit. We go to my bedroom, and I'm rubbing her back with lotion, her hips are shifting back and forth and I pull down her pants. Her right cheek has a little bit of hair on it, as if she had really light lumen-type hair there that she got in a habit of shaving, but she did a half-assed job. She doesn't take me seriously enough to put in more effort. I'm fingering her, she's squirting for a couple of minutes, and I say I'm tired. "Aw, I thought you were strong" she says, and she's starting to push my head down to her pussy. She's not really sexy as she's pushing on my head, and even though usually I really love giving oral sex I don't want to eat her out. My forearm is tired, and I'm laying back. She starts undoing my pants, misreading my exhaustion for wanting head. I'm completely soft as she's sucking, and the memory of chlamydia creeps back into my mind... no not again... And she starts to climb on top of me forcefully.

"I don't... I don't want to."

"I think you do."

"I don't have a condom."

"Well it looks like we'll have to without one." I don't want this anymore. As she's trying to take my limp cock inside of her with her hand, I grab her by the sides of her arms and throw her off of me. I'm telling her about how I had an STD, she grows noticeably uncomfortable, I'm ruining what was supposed to be a fun night. She no longer wants sex, but she's still horny. I get her off a few more times with fingering, a giant puddle beneath her, and she leaves without looking at me. I sit in my bed, and I weep uncontrollably.

On The Road To Recovery

I let a few weeks pass, reliving the realities of the gestation period of chlamydia and giving it time to be detected with a test. I'm in the same facility, marking my name again on a clipboard I never thought I'd hold again. I'm instinctively reaching into my pocket, searching for a Wellbutrin I no longer have. An older woman, who carries herself with obvious dignity is going over the routine with me. "So, what brought you in today?"

"Well... I was with someone that I don't know, and I'm worried because I had something before that... I'm scared I'll have it again."

"Did you have intercourse?"

"We didn't go all the way, just," and I almost whisper out of politeness, "oral sex. I stopped it before it went further than that."

"What do you think you would do in the future when meeting someone new?"

"I really, I just honestly want to be dating someone. But maybe it's like, I need to work on myself first."

She's nodding her head in agreement. "I think time spent on yourself is a good idea. I think what really helps me, and you should try, is time spent away from distractions—quiet places."

"I think sometimes about just throwing my cellphone away, it's stressful a lot of the time. It's so easy to talk to people, but at the same time, I'm usually not having conversations where much is being said." We've both written love letters, we've both driven with lovers and let the silence envelop each other, and we've both had the anxious buildup of not hearing from someone. There's something transcendent happening in our conversation. I'm seeing her as a beautiful person, older but with value, and she's looking at me with a kindness I can't remember. The phone call never comes to go back in for the cure, but I'm calling anyway to confirm, hoping somewhere to talk to that nice woman again.

I start thinking about Taylor throughout my days—how she said that if she could be with anyone, it would be me. I decide I have to tell her everything, and that I love her and nothing bad that happened between us matters anymore. I'm feeling invigorated. I've gathered up various gifts I had waiting for Taylor that I couldn't give to her, and I'm looking at socks in the mall. "She'd like these ones," I say to myself, and I buy them to add to the others. I'm driving to her work, a painting I'd done under one arm and holding onto a bag in the other hand. A portly gentleman in a suit comes out, saying, "You look like you're going to propose to someone!"

"I just might!" He can see it written all over me—I'm beaming with positivity. I'm looking up her name in the directory, calling up the number, and it's someone else on the line. She's moved to a different job, she says as I'm looking at her name on the directory—someone just hadn't updated it, and as always, I'm too late. I'm pounding my fists on my steering wheel as I'm crying in the parking lot. I regain composure and think to start driving to her house. My engine is feeling like it's not firing right in all cylinders, but just "Please hold on a little longer," I say out loud, praying to it, and to myself. I make it to her house, and I'm walking up to her door with the gifts. I knock, and the house is completely dark inside, but the door opens. "I'm looking for Tay-"

"She don't live here no more. If I knew where she was I'd tell you, but she's not here anymore."

"I see... Thank you..." I'm saying as the door is slammed in my face. A random girl I met on OkCupid sends me a snap of her ass, and it's about as perfect as it can be. "Oh yeah, that definitely needs my tongue inside it," I say.

"Yeah, come over, I want to fuck you."

I message back to her, "Okay, but do you

think that you could see anything in me... beyond just a hookup?"

"What do you mean?" She says back.

"Never mind." I say. When I'm driving back home, I realize that there must be a way to mimic a phone number, because people call and text on their iPads and other non-cellphones. I download an app that generates a new phone number, and I text Taylor. "Hey, this is Sean... I know you have my number blocked, and it's okay, I understand. I wouldn't be texting you if it wasn't important, but I just have to tell you some things."

"I did block you, but only because I started dating someone very controlling. I'm sorry."

"I understand, you do what you have to do to be happy. I went to your job today, hoping to find you, and I don't know, it just sort of happened. But they said you had left, and I looked so silly with all these gifts and things, but that's not why I'm texting you. I had this terrible thing happen a few months ago, where I got an STD, chlamydia. And it was so awful, I was so alone. And I thought about how you're a lot like me... and that you go into things very fast, and I just started to worry about you. I hate the idea of you having something, and maybe not knowing. And so, I felt compelled to go to you and talk with you, to make sure you're doing all right, because I love you very much. I always have, and I will always want the best for you." Like a dying man having an epiphany about how to live a life, I am too late, but I am at last sincere.

"I did leave that job, it just wasn't a good fit. As much as I'd like to accept the gifts, I don't think I can. I'm sorry to hear that about you, and I did have tests done this year, and luckily I am okay. I had to have my gallbladder removed, and they did a bunch of bloodwork as well. I wish I knew how to say the things that my heart feels... Can you give me your number, so that I can write it down? I may send a wayward message your way some day." Oh if only you knew my love, how I suffer that same affliction—of not knowing how to say the things that I feel!

　　"That's all I ever wanted, to know you're okay, and I know you have problems expressing yourself. I'm just so glad you're okay... and I hope wherever you are in the world and in your life... you'll be happy, and know that I'll always care for you." There's so much of me back there, with her, and always will be. It's not only the memory of her and the time we had together, but also the potential of greatness for her life—a greatness which I want her to achieve only for herself, that I love. I will try to reach out to her, over and over, to try and help her through her life path to reach that greatness. The stubborn part of her won't allow it, but that's also one of the reasons I'll continue to love her. I'm lucky enough to exist when and where I have, and I'm grateful to have ever met her. I'm thankful to the serendipitous stars that brought me to her, and if that feeling is as real as I believe it is in both of us, and we work on

312

ourselves, then maybe we will be ready for it if the stars bring us together again. For now she's living her own life, trying to find her own way, and that fills me with joy. I'm back home now, and I'm placing her gifts in my closet. Just like the teddy bear for my nephew, I know they will stay there collecting dust, but I need to believe that I can give them to her one day.

I'm back to my old job the next day, grateful that my boss took me back after my new job was the wrong fit. I'm washing dishes with a sixteen year old co-worker who's shy and nervous about being with her boyfriend for the first time. She asks me what will happen if she's no good at it, and I'm telling her what I wish someone had told me: "There's no shame in waiting. And if you love them, it's always good." Despite whatever wretched side effects and disasters may come in its wake, being lovers is always good in the moment— sometimes it takes a storm, filled with destruction and dreary hours, but also an eventual passing, to sharpen the hues and beauty of the horizon. I'm getting ready to leave for the day, it's snowing outside so I'm using the brush on my ice scraper to clear my car of snow. I'm heating it up, unsure of how many days it has left before it finally dies, wanting it to be warm for when I take another co-worker, Diana, home. I've grown quite fond of her, and while I'm taking her home, I'm telling her my thoughts, my hopes, and my fears. I'm at her house, and she's saying "thank you" for driving her home. I offer to walk down with her, or shovel her walkway, and she is politely refusing me. She's in her 60s, thin, and bundling her arms up into her chest as she slowly walks down her un-shoveled walkway. I'm watching every carefully measured step, and I'm waiting until she reaches her door and steps inside before I start to drive away. I've lost so much of myself, but it's these little exchanges, windows of real intimacy, that make me think maybe there is something still left inside me—something good.

Strength

I'm staring at my arm in the mirror at the gym, looking first at my flexed tricep, and then I'm gracefully moving into a bicep pose, trying to imitate the bodybuilder Ed Corny's graceful transitions. A young kid that goes to Red Land High school is asking me something, but it's hard to hear him over the music—something I used to need, but now I can focus without it. I ask him to repeat what he asked, and he's asking about the tattoo on my right arm. "That's Russian. It means sweetheart." I look back at myself in the mirror, looking at how far I've come. As I'm looking in the mirror, I'm seeing in the background far away the shy fat kid I once was—he'll be too slow to catch up to me for a long time. It's deadlifts and back today, which has become my favorite day in the gym. I'm warming up with 135 pounds, doing a Romanian deadlift, and I'm forcefully thrusting with my hips

315

on the lockout. I've been struggling with locking out my hips, and Romanians can help that problem by teaching how to properly load the hamstrings. I like not wearing a belt until I get to my heavy sets, and only this year started wearing one at all. As I'm putting on the next set of 45s, I'm feeling the Beta Alanine from my pre-workout rush through my body with a sharp tingling. 225 goes up smoothly, of course, and 315 feels so light. There was a time when 365 was my maximum weight. I like to do a double overhand grip (non-hook grip) on my warmup sets, to tax my grip in a way that can't be duplicated except by holding on to a heavy weight. I can also do 405 this same way with ease, and have done 455 pounds double overhand, as well. A girl walks by in leggings, and I catch a glimpse of her ass and she's going by the dumbbells, and I'm lifting 405 for reps with ease. I catch her looking at me in the mirror—quick glances at the weight and my upper back—and she thinks I can't see her looking. I'm loading it to 495 pounds, and I'm changing my grip to a switch grip, which prevents the barbell from rolling out of my hands by arresting rotation. It still doesn't feel heavy yet, so I set it to 585. I decide to hold off on the belt still, and this weight also flies up with ease. The girl leaves the area I'm in, and I leave to catch my breath and to see if those high school seniors are working out their asses on the abduction machine. They are here, but they're on a leg press machine (cable system, not plate loaded). I'm looking down the shorts of the blonde out of the corner of my eye as I walk toward the water fountain, although I don't drink anything because it tends to create gas in my stomach, and this is quite painful during a deadlift. As I leave the machine, I notice the MILF checking me out in the mirror and I smirk. On the way back I notice the brunette is on the machine now, and I'm doing a few reps on the standing calf raise machine to look at her crotch, a perfectly tiny camel toe is subtly showing through her leggings, and I feel indestructible and powerful.

I'm loading the bar to 615, and I put my weightlifting belt on for the first time. I couldn't figure out the balance between breath and bracing, while wearing a belt in the past, and still made it up to 605 pounds without it. Now it serves as a psychological confidence, in addition to the extra support. I'm very fast today, and 615 feels too light. I brought along my fractional plates, a nice item to have to prevent plateaus in training. I had learned of them while reading an article on strongmen, a lifelong obsession of mine, and how they used lead shot in their globe dumbbells to increase in such minute amounts that they built up their strength over years of tiny increases. I'm loading the barbell to 635 pounds, and putting on an extra four pounds with the fractionals, for a total of 639 pounds. I'm standing with the barbell over my midfoot. I take in a big breath to properly brace myself, breathing through my nose to avoid taking gulps of air to help prevent gas from forming. I raise my hands and then lower them in

318

such a way that I'm forcefully engaging my lats (latissimus dorsi muscles), and I'm bending over nearly stiff legged to grab the bar. This helps teach the way a hip hinge should feel, which is critical for a proper deadlift. I bend down and forward until my shins touch the bar, and then I explosively press the floor away from me to lift the weight off the floor. I'm struggling for a moment at my thighs to lockout—it's heavy, but I want it. I lock it out, and stand there a second before lowering the weight under control. I'm dizzy, seeing stars from the pressure of holding my breath, and I'm leaning up on the squat rack for balance. For a second, there is no music, and no one else there, and no pain— this is my quiet place. This is the most weight I can do, and so far, I have been natural—and I aim to keep it that way. I'm working more and more on myself with every new day, and I've barely scratched the surface. But I know that this too, all the pain and glory that brought me here, will be nothing more than a memory. Something to look back on, and laugh about how I was stuck there for so long, like 365 pounds.

One of the younger kids that looks up to me, wide-eyed and mystified, asks "Man, how did you get so strong?" I could tell you about Milo of Croton, picking up calves and walking with them as they grew into bulls, and how he had thought he could rip a tree a part with his hands, only to have his hubris be his downfall, as he became stuck and wolves ate him alive. I could tell you about Hermann Goerner, deadlifting 727 pounds with one hand. I could tell you about Paul Anderson, making his own bar for squatting with oil drums set to a thousand pounds, because he was too strong for his time. I could tell you about Arthur Saxon putting overhead 370 pounds in a bent press. I could tell you about Bill Kazmaier, completing his powerlifting competition in 1983 with a torn pectoral muscle to deadlift 799 pounds. I could tell you about Jón Páll Sigmursson, calling out to the Viking Gods, and I could tell you how he was lightning in a bottle as he burst the McGlashen stones off his chest in competition for the World's Strongest Man. I could tell you about Magnús Ver Magnússon continuing the Icelandic domination. I could tell you about Žydrūnas Savickas (Big Z) pressing 500 pounds overhead. I can tell you about Andy Bolton breaking the 1,000 pound deadlift barrier, and Benedikt Magnússon breaking that with 1,015, and Eddie Hall doing 1,018 with wraps and promising more on the horizon. I could tell you how David Gorman's *The Body Moveable* states that the biceps are strongest in the overhead position, as in chin-ups. I could describe to you the different forms of creatine, how the alkaline version is buffered and supposed to not break down into creatinine, and that this means it should be utilized more effectively. I could tell you about the function of ATP and sodium, and that carbohydrates are stored as glycogen in the muscles, and that high-intensity workouts are supposed to recruit more fast-twitch muscle fibers.

I could tell you how the muscles of the body work together, how the agonistic muscle is only as strong as the antagonistic muscle. But I can't tell you what it's like to have a love without expectation or obligation, one who would choose to be with me, even when I know I don't deserve it. That all I've ever known about love was a cheap substitute of strung-together casual encounters. And yet I keep going on, even though I'm alone, going off the hope that it's out there for me... And that this is what makes me strong.

I notice that it's a small crowd of younger guys before me, and I'm answering them. "Well, I would say showing up and being consistent is a big part of it. And keeping your stress down, eating enough." I start thinking about all the girls I've been with, and I'm starting to talk about something deeper. "And if I had to impart one thing on you guys, it's to take your time, and be patient. It will happen for you when the moment is right, if you keep going on." Keep going on, keep going on.

Over all these years and all those girls, I've given so much of myself away that it feels like some days there's nothing left. And when I'm so beat down and broken, I still recover, still fighting the tide. That's life, recovery and growth, and trying again and again. It doesn't matter how many times it doesn't pan out—what matters is the hope that it will. It's a terrible thing, to forever be a rebound. But I like to think of it more as being a stepping stone—that I'm leading those girls I've loved to better parts of their lives, and that they too, could be my stepping stones, leading me to that perfect person for me. Each passing second in life is an entirely different universe, where anything can happen, and even in the darkest parts of the galaxy, there is light traveling to it right now.

Within the hearts of every person, is a blueprint for who we will be in this life, and that blueprint is our soul. But this blueprint is incomplete, for the other half is in another person, and we're always searching for that other part of us. Yes, there are souls and soulmates, tiny incomplete portions of ourselves in the universe that take lifetimes to find one another. They sometimes make you the person you want to be, and they sometimes complete the person you are and there is no discernable difference between where you end and where they begin. And sometimes, they just make you feel like a normal person for the briefest of moments again, and you're only truly yourself with them. Instead of that one person, I've found many little pieces of the blueprint. They all were always meant to be a part of me, and I a part of them. Every single one of them mattered to me. It's easy to forget immense things, like that flowers don't work to be beautiful, they just are; that in our oceans are blue whales and eternal jellyfish; that birds just instinctively know to fly south in the winter; it's because these little drops of divinity are in our consciousness and all around us, that we overlook them. And with every new person we meet, we tap into this shared divinity, and I fit somewhere in that continuum of life in my own way... And all those girls that I'll never see again, save for in dreams and in pangs of nostalgia, behind all the lust, I loved them the only way I knew how—fast and hard, and with every ounce of sincerity I have. As much as I wanted the love to be returned, it never mattered that it wasn't—no one can tell you what to feel in your heart, who to love. I'll keep searching for my other, the idea of someone who was made as much for myself as I was for them is simply too wonderful to let go of. If beauty is in the eye of the beholder, then maybe ugliness is too. Maybe that match made in heaven will be able to see something worth loving in me. Maybe there's a place where I'm perfect—a home. Maybe that's enough of a reason to hold on, to keep going on. Maybe somewhere along the way, I can learn to be enough of a reason.

I'm finding that I'm getting stronger and recovering in ways I didn't think was possible. The darkness I've always seen on the horizon is receding, it's still there—but now when I look out, I see a glimmer of light overtaking it. I can almost see her in its radiance, and it's like I'm already in love with her and the world all at once. She could be in California watching the tide break on the coast. She could be a single mom whose child is her world. She could be a waitress at a restaurant. She could be a sweet stoner. She could be a woman who smiles shyly at me... It doesn't matter where she is, only that she exists and is out there, and I will never give up... A girl walks into the weight room, and I'm there too, and I feel so damn alive... Life is too fucking beautiful not to live it

www.ingramcontent.com/pod-product-compliance
Lightning Source LLC
Chambersburg PA
CBHW051328250626
47155CB00007B/2506